PROJECT WHORE

Andrea Lige-Saddler

Acknowledgments

I would like to start my thank you, praise and appreciation for God. Rose M. Gaulden-Harris, I thank you for life and my creativity. Through your death I found my purpose in life to write. To my sons'; my true source of strength. Devon Gaulden-Saddler, I thank you for showing me when having a great work ethic can take you; Tevon Gaulden-Saddler (twin); I want to thank you for teaching me the art of persistence of never giving up; Jayden Gaulden-Saddler, thank you for teaching me that not saying a lot, really makes a strong impact on not having to fight every battle. My sisters, Keli Gaines and Jackie Lige, thank you for your unconditional love and support. To My nieces Tiffany Gaulden-Campbell and Skyy Gaulden; for advice and encouragement to succeed regardless of my bumpy road. To my husband Vanness Saddler, I thank you for teaching me how to network or as you say" hustlin'." Chenel Banks, thank you, thank you, thank you for taking me under your wing and mentoring me in the publishing game.

Special Thanks

Veola Sanders Forbes, Demetri Gaulden-Sims, Legend Gaulden-Brown, Melissa Monfort-Mckay, Selina Braxton, Cherilyn Gee, Teresa Richardson, Tanya Johnson, Katina Maye, Ron Green, Henry Campbell, Brynne Ally, Madeline Tone and Albert Tone.

Chapter One

Keysha awoke in a haze. She turned over to a stranger lying beside her. Who was this big black nigger? She pulled back the comforter and his back is to her. He had a tattoo on his back, a heart with the name John in it. It must be his son, she thought. So he was obviously a great dad.

"What's this sticky shit on my face? Oh, hell no! This mug did not cum in my mouth and on my face!" she thought to herself.

Keysha was sitting on the side of her bed realizing how far she had actually come. From roaches to beautiful satin sheets and the sweet smells of scented candles instead of weed. To the expensive oak bedroom set from just any pieces of furniture she could get her hands on. She began to wonder what the hell had happened last night.

"Oh, yes. The party last night for my cousin, Monique, and I."

The man turned over and looked Keysha

in her face.   She smiled and looked him over
to see if she recognized him.   This man had an
s-curl, tattoos on his neck and amazing
eyebrows.   Keysha started to think to herself,
"Is he gay?"   It was those freshly plucked
eyebrows that made her wonder.

"Good morning," he said.

"Good morning to yourself."

"Okay, it's obvious you don't remember
what happened last night."

"I can see what happened.   It's all over
my face."

"Sorry about that.   We really got freaky
last night."

"Did we?   It's all a blur to me. I'm
sorry, but I hope I was good."

"Oh, that's a definite.   I would love to
be with you again.   You know, so it won't be a
blur to you."

"Maybe."

"Maybe, okay.   I hear that."

"Yes, maybe.   Damn, you look so
familiar."

"Are you still in a blur?"

"What?"

"Malcolm.   Davon's cousin."

"Oh, yeah, I remember you."

"I'm not like my cousin, so don't judge me," Malcolm stated.

"Good, because I can't stand your black-ass cousin."

"Oh, yeah, after last night, I know."

"Last night?" Keysha questioned.

"Yeah, last night."

"Oh, damn!   I remember.   Get up out of my bed so I can clean up and call Monique and apologize."

"Damn, okay.   Can I use your bathroom before you toss my ass out?"

"Yeah, yeah," Keysha mumbled.

"And Keysha, you are going to need more than just an apology."

"Yeah, I know."

Malcolm got up and walked into the bathroom, shutting the door behind him. Keysha stripped the bed of its sheets and replaced them with clean ones.   She began to pace back and forth, thinking about what had

happened last night.   She knocked on the bathroom door.

"Malcolm, put toothpaste on my toothbrush and hand it out to me, please."

The door opened briefly.   "Here you go."

"Thank you."

She went to use the other bathroom to scrub the hell out of her cum-stained face and brush her teeth.   Keysha could not believe she fucked one of Davon's cousins.   She hated him!   Keysha finished and came back to her room.   Malcolm was still in the bathroom.

"Today, Malcolm."

"I know you want me out.   Damn, can I wash my balls?"

Malcolm was in the bathroom trying to get the scent of fish off his dick.   He was damn near sick at the fact he had just fucked a female.   He could not go home to John like this.   He may have been a straight-up white boy, but he would fuck him up.   Keysha knocked on the door again.

"I'm almost finished," he called, then

whispered, "You nasty bitch."

"Hurry up.   Shit."

He opened the door and stepped out. Keysha had already made the bed, opened the windows and lit the candles.

"You don't waste any time.   I would have helped."

"Don't worry about I."

Keysha walked Malcolm to the door. She gives him a hug and a kiss.   Once on the other side, Malcolm began to scrub his lips with his hands.   He dug in his pockets and pulled out a breath mint.   Malcolm then pulled out his cell phone and dialed.

"What's up?"

"He, did you do that?"

"Yeah, man. I got her."

"Good.   Later."

"Later."

Back inside, Keysha started to replay all the events in her head from last night and began to wonder, does her cousin still love her? She began to think about what happened.

* * * * *

"Hey, girl, what's going on?" Keysha asked her cousin.

"Nothing but a bitch turning twenty-one.   I can drink legally now," Monique started laughing.

"Your ass has been drinking since you were twelve," Keysha reminded her.

"I know, but I've changed," she smiled.

"I know, you're a college graduate now."

"Don't knock college til you try it, Keysha Williams," she winked at her.

"Damn, Monique, not my government name.   Oh shit, here Davon comes.   I can't stand your boyfriend," Keysha rolled her eyes at her.

"I know, Keysha.   Be nice.   You are my favorite cousin," Monique pleaded.

"Yeah, yeah," Keysha said.

"Hey, Keysha," Davon spoke.

"Hello, Davon," Keysha said with such an attitude.

"Damn, all I said was 'hi'!   Why don't you bite my fucking head off?" he yelled.

"Don't tempt me," Keysha said, smiling

in his face.

Davon turned to Monique and said, "You better check your bitch-ass cousin."

"Nigga, who you calling a bitch? Your mother's a bitch!" Keysha screamed at the top of her lungs. "Trash-can nigga."

"Keysha, calm down. Not here at our party." Monique looked at her.

"You know what, Baby, I'm going over here with my cousin. If I were you, I would start inviting people with class instead of prostitutes." And on that note, he just walked away.

"Fuck you, you second-rate bastard." Davon just looked at her. He gave her the finger and laughed.

"Come on, Keysha. I hate when you and Davon argue. We are going to be family one day."

"Yeah, whatever."

Monique just glared at her, as if to say, please act right for me. She then reached into her pocked and pulled out a black and red box.

"I have a gift for you. Your birthday is

only a couple of days away."

She opened the box.   It was a diamond bracelet with a lion in it.

"That's right.   Respect the Leo," she yelled out.

Keysha reached behind the beige sectional sofa.

"I hope you like it."

"Oh shit, Kysh!   A mink jacket." Monique began to jump up and down. "Damn, are you fucking a millionaire now?"

"Yeah, something like that."   Keysha replied.

"Thank you, I love it!" Monique hugged her.

Monique ran over to show her man, Davon.   Once she got over there, he just shrugged his shoulders.   Keysha is so proud of her cousin.   Monique graduated from college. Her apartment is amazing!   She loves the way Monique has neutral colors with splashes of vibrant colors throughout.   And that beautiful fire place with the picture Keysha adores.   It is a naked black man holding a black woman

above his head.   Keysha likes the symbolism of strength.

"Yeah, be mad, Bitch!   Because you're broke ass couldn't afford anything that special!"

"Hey, wait a minute, that's my song they're playing," Keysha thought.

Keysha got on the floor and started to get her dance on.   The Monique joined her. Next thing they knew, everyone was dancing. People were coming over and handing Monique and Keysha birthday drinks galore. Keysha's head was spinning.   She staggered into the kitchen to get something to eat.

Monique's kitchen was black, white and red.   All Moe's appliances were black and her accent rugs were red.   It was a nice kitchen, everything went together.   Keysha walked to the kitchen where her ant was fixing herself a plate.

"Hi, Auntie Jackie," Keysha slurred.

"Hi, yourself, drunk-butt," she laughed.

"Yeah, I have had one too many."

"So you will get someone to take you

home?" Auntie questioned.

"Of course I will," she replied reassuringly.

"Happy Early-Birthday, Kysh," Auntie said.

"Thank you."

"How's my niece doing?"

"Fine."

"How is your mother?"

"She's fine also. You should call her."

"No, I don't think so."

"Auntie, it's been eight years!"

"Keysha, your mother is....no, I don't want to talk bad about her. Let's just leave it like it is," she smiled at her.

"Well, life is too short, Auntie," Keysha said.

"Yes, it is. That's why I'm taking my food and getting back to Harmony and CSI." She headed for the door.

"Bye, I'll see you soon, Auntie.

"You better."

Just when Auntie was about to head back upstairs, Monique walked through the

kitchen door.

"What? A secret meeting with your own daughter?" Monique slurred.

"No, Nosey," Jackie said, "I just came down for a plate of food."

"Of course, Mom," Monique said. "Is Harmony asleep?"

"You know your daughter is a night owl."

"Monique, we have to get our mothers' talking to each other again," Keysha pleaded.

"Yeah, and it snows in the middle of August in Georgia," Monique laughed.

"Look, I'm leaving on that note. Monique, make sure your cousin gets home safely."

"I will, Mom."

"Keysha, make sure you bring Treasure over tomorrow. Harmony misses her," she said.

"I will definitely do that," Keysha said.

Monique and Keysha returned to the party. As soon as they stepped into the room, the music stopped playing. Davon was standing

in the middle of the floor with his hand out. Monique walked over to him, looking back at Keysha, smiling. Keysha hunched her shoulders as if to say, I don't know what's going on, and she really didn't. Davon got down on one knee.

"Oh, hell fuckin' no," Keysha said to herself.

She knew Monique wanted to marry that fool, but was it actually going to happen? This is what that nigga said to Keysha's favorite cousin, hell, her only cousin.

"Moe, you know we've been together since high school. We also have a beautiful daughter together, and I never want to wake up to anyone else but you in the morning."

The party-goers began to sigh and aww.

"That's why I want to make you mine forever. Will you marry me, Baby?"

Monique looked at Keysha with a huge smile on her face. Keysha thought to herself, "Oh hell no, not today." Actually, she said it aloud by accident, being drunk and all. You know what they say. A drunken heart speaks

a sober mind.   Oh hell, you say what you really want.   Everyone turned around and looked at her.

"Shut the hell up, Bitch!" Davon said.

"No, you shut up.   You're not good enough for my cousin," Keysha replied.

"Keysha, please, do not show your ass tonight!" Monique yelled.

Everyone began to gather their thing, set to leave, when Davon did the unthinkable.   He hauled off and slapped Keysha in the face.   She was stunned for a minute.   Suddenly awakened, she kicked him the balls and banged him in the face.   His ass went down with the quickness.

"Please, stop now, Goddamn it!" Monique cried.   They both just stood there looking at each other, huffing and puffing.

Davon and Keysha were standing there; she with her eye throbbing and him with his nose bleeding.

"Can someone please take my cousin home?   She has had too much to drink," Monique begged.

"No, I haven't!"

"Keysha, shut the fuck up!"

Keysha was shocked and a little scared because Monique rarely got upset.

Keysha looked around the apartment and there was glass, drinks, and blood everywhere.

"Yeah, Bitch, bounce!" Davon said.

"Bitch?   Oh really? Let's tell Moe about some of the shit you've done!"

They began to argue again.   Some of the people from the party were still there, making sure not to miss any of the scoop.

"Oh no, the two of you want to start this shit again? I just want to thank the both of you for ruining my party.   Now get the fuck out!" Monique went to her room and shut the door behind her.

"Hey, Keysha.   I'll take you home," a voice said.

"Thank you!"

Davon began to clean up the mess in the living room.   After cleaning, he looked around and saw the little velvet box on the floor with

the ring in it.   He picked it up and went toward the bedroom door.   Davon knocked but got no response.   He called out to Monique but still no answer.   Davon turned the doorknob and walked in.

The shower was running, so he took off his clothes.   He hoped that Monique would let him join her.   He walked into the steamy bathroom, bringing the ring with him.   Their room was beautiful: the Egyptian comforter, pillows in every color, cool warm tan on the walls, along with authentic African art work. Davon lit some candles.

"Monique, can I join you?" Davon asked.

"Umm, I don't think so," she replied.

"Baby, please," he begged.

"Baby, nothing.   You and Keysha act like damn animals."

"Keysha did," he said.

"No, you and Keysha!" Monique told him.

"You're right.   I need to be a man and ignore your cousin."

"Yeah, I know," she rolled her eyes at

him.   "Look, I love my cousin, but I love you, too."

"Baby, I love you, too"

"Prove it, then."

"How?" asked Davon.

"Put whatever problems you and Keysha have in the past.   For me."

"Yes, I can do that for you, but your cousin?"

"Don't worry about Keysha.   I'll talk to her."

"Can I get in the shower now?"

"Yes, I guess so.   Everybody has to wash."

"Where are you going?"

"I'm finished," she smiled.

"Wait one minute."   He got down on his knee, water hitting him in the face.

"What's your answer?"

She stood there and paused for a minute, which seemed to feel like hours to Davon.

"Yes, Davon."

He took the ring out of the box and

threw the box on the floor.   Then he put the
ring on her finger.   She started to bend down
to kiss him, but he stopped her.

"What's the matter?"

"Nothing.   Since I am already on my
knees, I may as well eat that pussy."

"Yeah, you should," Monique smiled.

Davon put one of Monique's legs on the
side of the tub.   He then spread her lips apart
and stuck his tongue inside her.   Monique
began to moan, which turned Davon on even
more.   He stood up and slammed her back
against the shower wall.

"Damn, Baby.   Do you want me?"

"Oh, shit.   Hell yeah, Moe!"

"Well, take this ass and do what you
want with it."

"Anything?" he asked.

"Anything."

He picked Monique up, opened her legs,
and put his hard dick inside her.   She liked
that shit!   Next, he took her to the bed and
told her to get on all fours.   She noticed the
candles lit all over the room.   Davon had

planned this.   He grabbed her, pulling hair and slapping her on the ass.   He inserted himself into her.   Davon seemed like an animal.   They were both drunk as hell and extremely horny.   This made their sex seem explosive.   On this night, he treated her like a whore, and she liked the feeling.   They were both breathing hard and Davon finally came. He just laid there.

"Damn, Hon.   You were like an animal tonight.   I liked that shit," she told him.

"I like the fact that you let me pull your hair.   I know you don't like to try new things," he said.

"Well, maybe I'm changing.   Damn, I'm sticky.   I'm going to take a shower.   Are you coming?" she asked.

"Yeah, in a minute."

Monique walked over to the bathroom door.   She looked back at the bed; the bedspread and sheets were everywhere. Davon had a serious look on his face.   What he was thinking, she wondered. Lying in bed, Davon started thinking about how he couldn't

stand that bitch, Keysha.

"I'll get that meddling bitch, yet," he said to himself as he reached for the phone and made a call.   He then got up and joined Monique for a shower.

* * * * *

The next day the phone rang and Keysha picked it up.   It was Monique.   She didn't think Monique would talk to her again after the fiasco last night.

"Hello?" I said.

"Hello yourself. Are you sober this morning or do I need to call back later?" Monique asked.

"No, you don't have to call back.   I'm okay."

"Well, your ass wasn't alright last night. You acted like a Goddamn fool!"

"Yes, Monique, I know.   I want to apologize for that."

"Oh, no, there is no reason to be sorry, just yet."

The tone in Monique's voice made her feel a little uneasy.   She could tell Monique

was still very upset with her.

"What do you mean, just yet?"

"You are my best friend and my only cousin, right?"

"Yes, I am.   You are always going to be my best friend."

"Well, as my best friend and only cousin, respect my decision to be with Davon."

"I can't stand his ass!   He is no good for you!"

"To be honest with you, Keysha, you don't have to like him, I do.   The two of you do have to be cordial to each other.   The both of you are special to me.   I've already spoken to Davon, and he has agreed to make an effort and so should you."

There was a long pause on the phone. Keysha really didn't want to give in, but she loved her cousin.

"Because if you can't, tough.   I have already accepted his proposal."

"Well, what can I say?"

"You can say, I'm happy for you.   I have your back, like I always have had yours,

regardless of what everyone says about you. I don't care because I know you and love you for you, not what you can give or do for me."

"You're right and I am sorry for not having your back."

"So, will you be my maid-of-honor?"

"Yes, I'll be your maid-of-honor."

"Try not to be too happy about it."

"I said I would try. It's not going to happen overnight."

"The fact that you're trying is good enough for me."

"Well, do you think we can have lunch today?

"Yes, I think that would be great. I have to tell you what I woke up to this morning, or rather who I woke up to!"

"Oh, my goodness. Well, meet me at our regular place at one."

Chapter Two

Life in the projects was all Keysha ever really knew; people getting shot, drugs and murder. She stood at the back of the low-income townhouse. She looked just beyond her backyard; all she could see were trash and drug needles. Keysha wished she could live somewhere else. No more worrying about that today because it's her fourteenth birthday. Actually, it's her cousin Monique's birthday, too. This was the best summer ever. Keysha had a birthday party and she would start high school on Monday. She finished putting the pink balloons everywhere. She made one final look around to make sure everything was right. Keysha turned and noticed her mother flirting with the neighbor, Mr. Jones. Keysha's mother, Pam Williams, is a five-foot-four, light-skinned, brown-eyed nut. There she was, standing in her halter top and booty shorts. Her mother was commanding attention as usual.

Her favorite aunt and cousin had arrived. They pulled up in her aunt's red Hyundai Sonata. Keysha's Auntie Jackie is five-foot-six, with long black hair and a great body that she is always covering up. Jackie walked in the gate and Keysha ran over and hugged her. Jackie handed her a beautifully wrapped gift.

"Happy Birthday, gorgeous," her aunt said.

"Thank you, Auntie."

Her aunt started over to the table where the grown-ups were playing cards.

"Hello, Pam," Jackie said.

"Hello to yourself, Jackie," Pam replied. "Hi, Monique."

"Hi, Auntie," Monique said.

Monique hugged her aunt and Pam gave her a gift.

"I hope you like."

"I like anything you give me, Auntie," Monique said.

"Why don't you girls go over and look at the decorations. Go and talk to your friends."

The backyard had balloons, streamers and barbeque smoke everywhere.

"Hey, there's Tameka." We went over to speak to her. Coming in right behind Tameka were Shaniqua, Trina, Leslie and Michelle.

"What's up, Girls?" Monique and Keysha asked.

"Hey!" the girls replied.

"Are y'all hungry," Keysha asked.

"You know we are, Girl," Tameka blurted out.

"Put the presents on the table," Monique laughed.

They walked over to the table. There were collard greens, macaroni and cheese, ham and deviled eggs. It was a soul-food buffet.

"Dang, Girl, your mom sure can throw down!" Trina remarked.

The girls piled their plates, sat down and began to grub. Keysha looked up to see her mom over at the cooler. She looked at Monique, who was already glancing her way. They were both thinking the same thing.

Please, let that be a soda she was reaching for...but of course, it was not.   Pam headed in Jackie's direction.   Jackie was opening the gate for Keysha's Uncle Gerald.   Jackie and Gerald weren't married, but he was her cousin's father, so she thought of him like an uncle.

"It's about time you make it," Jackie said.

"Where's my girl?" Gerald asked.

"She's over there with Keysha and please thank Pam for the party," Jackie replied.

"Let's hope she doesn't act like a damn fool today," he said as he glanced in her direction.

"Let's.   Here she comes," Jackie said.

Pam came toward the two of them, staggering.   She was slurring, trying to get her speech together.

"Well, hello Gerald.   Can a sista get a hug?" Pam said with a drunken grin on her face.

Now Gerald was definitely a catch. Gerald was six-four with a medium build and

he was black, well-dressed and educated. He was gorgeous. He also was a business man. He had his own clothing store.

"Of course, Pam," he hugged her. "Thank you for throwing the party for my little girl."

"No problem. I love my niece," Pam said.

At this time, Monique and Keysha thought it was a great time to go over and say hello. Keysha could feel a disaster ready to happen. Monique ran over to give her dad a big hug. He wrapped his manly arms around his petite daughter. Keysha felt a little jealous. She never knew her father. Pam probably didn't even know who he was. They never talked about it.

"Hi, Daddy," Monique said.

"Hi, Angel. Happy Birthday!" he answered.

"Thanks, Daddy," Monique smiled.

"Hey, Keysha. I didn't forget you," Gerald said as he turned to her.

"Hi, Uncle Gerald," Keysha said.

"I have something for you girls."

He pulled out two identical boxes: one for Monique and one for Keysha.

"Well, since you're opening gifts, let's go over to the table and open the rest," Pam suggested.

Everyone gathered around the table to watch them open their gifts.   Keysha's first present was from her mother.   It was a CD player and Jay-Z's new CD.   Monique opened her gift from her aunt and it was the same.

"Thank you, Auntie.   I love it!" Monique said.

"You're welcome, Monique-baby," Pam told her.

"Yeah, thank you, Mom.   You know Jay-Z's my man," I laughed.

Next they opened their gifts from Jackie. She had given Monique and Keysha two hundred-dollar gift certificates to the mall.

"I didn't know what kind of clothes to get the both of you," she said.

"We do!" Monique and Keysha quickly answered together, laughing.

"Thank you, Auntie Jackie," Keysha said.

"Thank you, Mommy," Monique said.

The gift from Uncle Gerald was next. He instructed the girls to open them at the same time. The boxes were wrapped in red velvet paper with white bows. Once they were opened, Keysha and Monique were stunned at what they saw. They were gold necklaces with their names in them. They both jumped up and down.

"Everyone has these!" Keysha said.

"Girl, we are everybody's' now!" Monique screamed.

The girls ran over and gave him a great big hug. Keysha and Monique headed over to their girlfriends to brag. The girls were oohing and ahhing. Then they heard Keysha's mother's mouth. Everyone was staring in her direction.

"There you go again with that shit!" Jackie said.

"Keysha is not going to live with your stuck-up ass!"

"I was just trying to help you out, so that you can get yourself a career with benefits and..." Pam cut her off mid-sentence.

"My life is just fine, Bitch, and I don't need your fucking pity!"

There was a crowd starting to gather around them, but this didn't seem to matter to Pam.

"You know what?   Let's not do this at the kids' party," Jackie said.

"This is my mother-fucking house, Jackie.   And I'll say what I want!   See, you don't run shit over here with your better-than-thou attitude!"

"You know what?   I never considered myself to be better than you.   But if that's the way you feel, then I am better than you!"

"Bitch!   Jackie, you know I'll lace your ass," Pam said in a drunken voice.   "You were always Mommy's favorite!"

"Pam, you're drunk.   Cut this shit out...the kids..." Gerald said.

"Gerald, nigga, who do you think you're talking to?   As a matter of fact, did you tell

Jackie that I fucked you before?" Pam blurted out.

Everyone's mouths fell open. Keysha was so embarrassed. She looked over at Monique who had tears in her eyes. Keysha grabbed her hand.

"Moe, I'm so sorry."

"Don't worry about it, Keysha," Monique said, just as Pam started in on Jackie again.

"Well, did he tell you that, Jackie? Did he?" she said.

"Yes, he did, Pam. That is why we are not together, because I told him a man could come and go, but my love for my sister was forever."

Pam just looked stunned. Jackie looked like she was about to dig up in that ass. Hell, so did Keysha and Monique. Jackie had a killer look in her eyes.

"Bitch, please save that shit for someone who cares."

"Monique, let's go," Jackie said.

"She doesn't have to go anywhere," Pam said.

"Let me say something you once said to me. This is my goddamned daughter!" Jackie said, staring straight into her face.

"Whatever, Bitch!" Pam said as she walked into the house.

Jackie went over to Keysha and put her head in her hands. Keysha was crying the whole time they were arguing. Jackie told Keysha that she would always be welcome in her life and home. She also said that the disagreements between her mother and aunt should not affect her relationship with Monique. She kissed her on the forehead. She noticed her favorite uncle and cousin were walking out the gate to their car. Keysha turned around and saw that everyone had left.

She went into the house to ask her mother why she would do that on her special day. She grabbed the door hard and slammed it. There was no response from her mother. She thought for sure that Pam would cuss her out. She stormed through the kitchen and into the living room. There was no one to be found. Keysha headed upstairs toward to her

mom's room.   She began to feel scared.   She
didn't really know what to expect. Was she
going to get cussed out?   Keysha reached for
the room door and peaked in.   She was passed
out in bed.   Her clothes were thrown over the
suede chaise lounge.   Keysha began to cry.
She wanted a normal mother, not a crazy one.

Keysha went back to the yard to get her
CD player and other gifts.   She also got herself
a plate of food to take back upstairs to her
room.   Keysha stopped in the kitchen to get a
soda.   She glanced at her high school schedule
on the refrigerator.

"Hey, Keysha, are you alright?" a
familiar voice said.   She looked up from the
refrigerator to see her mother's boyfriend,
James.

"Yes, I guess so."

"Don't worry about your mom.   She
had too much to drink," he said.

"I'm just upset because she'll get up
tomorrow and act like nothing happened and
won't even apologize to me for ruining my
birthday party."

"I know. You're right about that. So what are you about to do?"

"I'm going to my room to listen to my music and eat."

"You need any help?"

"No, thank you."

Keysha went toward the doorway that lead upstairs. James did the weirdest thing to her.

"Try not to be too upset," he said and then smacked her on the behind. Keysha looked at him like he was crazy. He just walked outside and shut the door. When she got to her room, Keysha put her food on the nightstand, along with her soda. She tossed the CD player and her new CD on the bed. She pulled open the dresser drawer to get her Mariah Carey CD. It always made her feel better. She jumped on the bed and popped the CD into her headset and put on the headphones. Keysha was chewing and singing at the same time. On the fourth song she began to doze off when Pam suddenly came into the room. She needed Keysha to help

clean up the leftovers and decorations from the party.

After carrying everything from the backyard into the kitchen and helping get the decorations down, Keysha was sleepy.

"I'm going to take a shower and go to bed."

Keysha was at the bottom of the stairs, looking up and feeling too weak to make it to the top. She glanced out of the corner of her eye. Her mother and James were sitting on the sofa watching TV. She contemplated staying downstairs, but decided to go ahead and turn in for the night.

She felt like a new person after washing all her troubles away. She could hear her bed calling her. All that was left to do was say goodnight to her mother and James. As she reached her bottom step, Keysha yelled to her mom and James goodnight. Her mother motioned for Keysha to come over toward her.

"I can't get a kiss goodnight?" her mom said. She reached down to kiss her. Thank God she had sobered up. Keysha leaned in to

give James a kiss.   He was the only father she had ever known.   Suddenly, James reached out and grabbed her breast.

"They're growing," he said.

She glanced at her mom.   "Go ahead and show him."

"No, Mommy."

James turned to her mother and said that he would give her fifty dollars for a look. He had this dirty-old-man look on his face.

"Girl, hurry up! We can use that money to get your hair and nails done for school."

"Mommy!"

"God damn it, Keysha!"

Keysha did not want to make her mad so she did what she was asking.   She pulled up her shirt and stood in front of James.   He began to feel on himself.   Keysha pulled her shirt down and walked away.   James reached in his pocket to grab his wallet and gave her mom fifty dollars.

"Keysha, wait.   Come and get your money," her mom said to her.

"I don't want it."

"Come and get it.   You earned it."
Keysha went back to the sofa and took her
money.

"Wait, do you want to make more
money?" James smiled at Keysha, in that same
dirty-old-man way.

"No, thank you."

"Wait one fucking minute, missy.   I
make the decisions in this house."

"Mommy, please.   Nothing else.   I'm
tired and want to go to bed."

Her mom turned to James.   "She's not
going to suck your dick.   Keysha's too young
for that."

Keysha could not believe what she was
hearing.   Her mom was pimping her out!

"I just want her to sit on my lap."

"What?   Mommy, no!"

"How much money are we talking about,
James?"

"One hundred fifty dollars."

"Keysha, go over and sit on his lap," she
said, matter-of-factly.

James took the money out.   "Here,

Pam."

Pam took the money and stuck it in her bra.   Then she yelled at Keysha because she hadn't yet moved.   Keysha felt like she was frozen.

"Come on now, Keysha!"

"Mommy, no!"

Pam jumped up and slapped the hell out of her.   "I don't know who the hell you think you're yelling at!   The hell you won't go over there and sit on his lap.   You will help out around this house."

She was so scared to do it, but more afraid of her mother.   Pam had never hit Keysha in her entire life.   She walked over and sat on James's lap.   He began to moan and move his hips back and forth.   He put his hands on her breasts and squeezed them gently.   Keysha looked over at her mom, but she was counting the money she had just been given.   Keysha wanted to cry, but then she began to enjoy it.   James's penis began to rise and then it was rock hard.   She jumped up.

"Enough!"

"Okay, James. Enough," Pam said.

Keysha ran to her room and locked her door. She lay in her bed thinking herself that her mother was crazy. Pam couldn't care less about her. There was a knock on the door. Keysha's room is purple and pink. There was a big stuffed pillow in the shape of lips, a Strawberry Shortcake Doll on her bed, Bow Wow posters on the walls and a neon pink phone.

"Go away!" Keysha yelled.

"Keysha, open this door right now!"

She jumped up and ran to her door. After being slapped earlier, she didn't want a repeat performance.

"Keysha, I know you're mad, but you have to understand I need you to help out with the bills. You need things I can't sometimes provide you with. I also want some nice things."

"Mommy, I love you, but I'm scared."

"Keysha, you will get over that. Believe me. It feels good."

Keysha just stared at her. "What feels

good?"

"Having sex with a man or a woman."

"Ugh!   That is nasty.   You know, being with a woman?"

"Nasty or not, you have to pull your weight around her."

Keysha sat there in silence, sure that something else was going on.

"Keysha, I need you to do me a favor."

"Mommy, what now?"   She was thinking to herself, wasn't James feeling me up enough?

"James is going to pay me five hundred dollars to have sex with you."

"Oh, hell no!"

"What did you say?"

"Mommy, I'm not talking to you.   I'm just scared.   I have never had sex before and James is like my dad!   He's the only father I've known for the last six years."

"Well, he's not your father, so don't feel bad about it."

"I won't do it with him, ever.   He can just forget it. I don't care how much money he

is giving you."

"Oh, yes, you are, and yes, you will. James just went to the ATM. When he returns he is coming up here. Here, take this."

"What is this, Mom?"

"A condom. Always use them. On Monday I'm taking you to the clinic to get you on the Pill. We need money, but we don't need any babies."

"Mommy, please don't make me do it!"

"Baby, it's time for you to grow up. Do what he says and he will be gentle." She got up and walked out the door.

Pam sat on the front steps. The Georgia heat was crazy. It was hotter in the house than outside, and of course, all the crack heads were out walking around. The cock roaches were everywhere; those bitches can fly, too. James came toward the house with a big grin on his face.

"Did you get the money?" she asked him.

"Here, I have five hundred dollars," he smiled at her.

"Okay, now sit your ass down. Let's go over some rules. First, this is her first time," Pam explained.

"Yeah, right!" he laughed.

"James, don't fuck with me. She's not on the Pill, so use a condom. Nothing rough and don't kiss her on the mouth," she instructed.

"Okay. Anything else?" James asked.

"Also, leave two hundred dollars on the nightstand when you're done."

"Okay, Pam, I get it. If everything goes well, this could be a weekly thing," he smiled.

"That will be up to Keysha. Oh, yeah, you hurt my daughter, and I'll kill you," Pam told him.

Keysha was lying in bed, nervous as hell, clutching her Strawberry Shortcake Doll. She could not believe her mother. She was right, Keysha thought. Pam had been taking care of her all by herself. Keysha needed to do her share. She thought she was ready. There was knock at the door.

"It's me, James.

She sat up on the bed. "Come in," she said nervously.

James stood there in his Sunday best, with a fresh new cut.. He appeared to be nervous as well.

"Hey, I need to talk with you first. Your mother gave me some rules. Do you have a condom?" he asked.

"Yes."

"I can't kiss you on the mouth. And I'm not going to hurt you."

She relaxed a little. "So, what do we do first?"

"Let's start by taking off our clothes," he said.

They both started to undress. Keysha was a little uncomfortable this was the man she considered her father.

"Keysha, can I put my tongue inside you?"

"Are you supposed to?"

"It will relax you."

Keysha leaned back and opened her legs a little. "I need you to open your legs a little

wider than that."

So she did. James then spread her lips apart and not the ones to her mouth. He stuck his wet, hot tongue inside her vagina. To Keysha's surprise, it felt good. She started to moan. James looked up at her.

"I like the taste of you pussy."

"Do you now? Then why are you talking to me? Get back to tasting."

James returned to relaxing her. He flipped her on her back and started licking her ass. Was this normal, she wondered. She didn't care. It felt so good. So Keysha decided to go with the flow. He turned her back over and began sucking and squeezing her breasts. She loved thi feeling she was beginning to have.

"Are you okay?" James asked.

"Oh, yes," she moaned.

He continued to try and please her. Keysha didn't know anything about sex, so it was all pleasing her. He then stuck his dick inside her. It felt good. She began to move her hips back and forth. She thought to herself,

she could take a dick if it felt like this.

"If you like that, then you'll love this."

He grabbed the condom and put it on. He laid on top of her. He pressed and pressed against her thighs. He finally got in. It didn't feel like before. This thing was bigger. She felt so stupid. It was his finger inside her the first time, not his dick. This definitely feels different than a finger. It was painful at first, but pleasure was shortly behind. James told her to move her hips around. He said it would feel better. She did and he was right. Then he put her legs on his shoulders and went deep. Keysha screamed.

"I'm sorry. You're not ready for that yet."

He continued for another fifteen minutes. Then he got up. Keysha just lay there, quiet. He reached into his wallet and gave her three hundred dollars.

"Tell you mother I gave you two hundred," he smiled at her.

"Okay."

He put his clothes and stared at the bed.

"That blood right there is normal when you first start having sex."

She was so embarrassed. Keysha looked down at the sheets and pulled the covers up to her neck. The door slammed and she continued to lay there. She couldn't believe she wasn't a virgin anymore. Then her door opened slowly.

"Keysha, get up. Change your sheets and take a shower," Pam said. Then she closed the door.

Chapter 3

Damn, it's six o'clock already! Keysha moved the empty bubble gum wrappers out of the way to turn the alarm clock off. She got up and went over to the closet to pick out something for school. Keysha glanced out the window to see the sun already beaming. It will be another hot day. A nice short skirt today, she thought. She picked out a pink skirt and a white halter top with pink sling backs. Keysha headed to the bathroom to brush her teeth and wash her face and accidentally walk in on James using the bathroom. She jumped back.

"I'm sorry for walking in on you," Keysha said.

"It's nothing you haven't seen before," he smiled at her. "And you most likely will see it again." He shook his penis off and motioned her to come into the bathroom with him. Keysha walked in and headed for the sink to wash her face and brush her teeth. Keysha grabbed her toothbrush, toothpaste and turned on the water. All of a sudden she felt warm

funky breath on the back of her neck.

"I need to wash my hands," James smiled

"I can move out of your way," Keysha quickly said

"Are you alright?" he asked.

He reached around her waist to wash his hands. James began to grind on her butt. She could feel him getting hard. He started to breathe faster while moaning. Keysha thought, not again. Please not before school. James grabbed her breast and was now humping her like he did in the bed. Next he lifted up her shirt and grabbed Keysha's breasts. Her breasts were now soapy and slippery.

"Keysha, are you up for school?" Pam yelled down the hallway.

"Yes, I am, Mom."

James quickly stopped caressing her breasts and ran down the stairs. Keysha looked down at her shirt that was now soaking wet. She looked in the mirror; there was crust in her eyes, a scarf on her head and a mud mask. Keysha just stood there and stared in the

mirror until she heard her mom.

"Today, Keysha!" her mom yelled.

She returned to brushing her teeth and cleaning her face. Keysha went back to her room and locked the door. Keysha made her bed right away, so she didn't forget and get grounded for it. Pam was a stickler for neatness. She threw her nightclothes on the freshly made bed and stood in front of the mirror. Keysha quickly grab her night clothes and put them in the drawer.

Keysha looked at herself: 5'2", caramel skin and a head full of micro braids. She didn't look any different. She looked at the clock.

"Oh shit! It's 6:58 am. I'm going to be late my first day of high school. Mom, I'm going to need a ride," Keysha yelled down the stairs.

"Aw shit, Keysha. James is going to have to take you," she yelled back up to her. Keysha's stomach began to hurt.

"Mom, come here for a minute, please," she yelled.

"What, Keysha?" she said as she came

up the stairs.

"I don't want to go with James."

"Why not, Keysha?"

"Because you know why, Mom."

"Look that was Saturday. Today is Monday. If he tries to touch you without paying, say, 'Hell no, Nigga. Where da money at?'" Then she started laughing. "Keysha, hurry up, please."

"But Mommy."

"Keysha, 'but' nothing. Did he hurt you? If he did, I'll kill him."

"No, but..."

"Okay then. I have to do something for Mr. and Mrs. Jones before they go to work."

On that note she walked out. Keysha grabbed her notebook and purse. First day of high school and she was going to be late. She ran down the stairs. James was already in the car, and so was her mom.

"I thought you had to go over to Mr. and Mrs. Jones."

"I'll do it later, Scared Ass."

Keysha was so relieved to see her in the

car. Just as she was about to get in the car she heard a horn. It was her Aunt Jackie.

"Hey, Cuz." Monique said, "I see I'm not the only one late today."

"You know it takes time to get cute," Keysha smiled.

"Hi, Stinky Butt," Auntie Jackie says to Keysha.

"Hi, Auntie." She walked over to her aunt's side of the car.

"Do you want to ride with Monique and me?"

"Can I, Mom?"

"I don't give a damn," she said to me. "Just don't be late to school."

Keysha jumped in the car and they pulled off. She looked back. She saw her mom and James go over to the Jones' house. Keysha thought to herself, 'What are they going to do?'

"Are you girls ready for school?" My aunt's eyes are in the rear view mirror.

"Oh, definitely," I said. Keysha checked Monique over. Her cousin was 5"4, with pretty skin, light brown eyes, very long red hair, and

she was very skinny.

"I can't believe you dyed your hair red," I said to Monique.

"Does it look right, Keysha?"

"Yes, it looks bananas, in a good way."

"What is 'bananas'?" my aunt asked. We laughed at her and told her it meant crazy in a good way.

"You young people and your crazy language!"

Finally they were in front of the school and stepped out of the car. The last bell rang. All you saw were new students running past lockers, looking scared and lost. You knew those were freshmen. Monique and Keysha ran to the building to head to class. When they stepped into the building, they zoned in on a gorgeous boy standing in the hallway. This boy was tall with caramel skin and green-grey eyes. They looked at each other and said simultaneously, "He is mine!" They started laughing.

"I'll see you at lunch, okay?" Monique said

"See ya," she said.

First period was health class for Keysha, and she was late. The teacher waved her in and she sat down. Keysha was happy the teacher did not embarrass her.

The teacher was going over class rules and procedures when there was a knock at the door. Oh shit, it's the cutie from earlier.

"Hi, Mrs. Miller," the boy said.

"Well, well...Davon Brach. I'm glad to see that you decided to join us," Mrs. Miller said.

Davon Brach...Damn, this nigga is fine. He looked her way and smiled.

"I got lost." He said

"Really, Davon, you're a junior. I think you know your way around this school."

"C'mon, Mrs. Miller, cut me some slack."

"I will in after school detention." And she handed him a detention slip.

The bell rang and Keysha gathered her books and headed to her next class.

"Excuse me," the voice said. She turned around and it was Davon Brach.

"Yeah, what's up?" She said trying to sound older.

"Damn, you look good as shit."

"Thank you."

"Can I ask you a question?"

Keysha thought to herself, 'You can ask me anything you want to. The answer will always be yes.'

"That girl you were with earlier, does she have a man?"

No the fuck he didn't. He liked Monique. "Oh, yeah, that's my cousin."

"Can you hook me up and give her this number?" Davon asked.

"Yeah, sure I can." My feelings were hurt. "What is your name?"

"Davon Brach, shorty," he said.

He turned away and Keysha went off to her next class. Sitting in class, she was happy the day was half over. Keysha's mind was on lunch, which was in ten minutes. Her stomach started to growl. She wanted it to hurry up. Finally the bell rang and she tore out of Spanish class. Once Keysha reached the

cafeteria, she saw that Monique had saved her a seat. She waved at her and went straight to the lunch line. Keysha got her food and headed to the table. By the time she got there, Trina and Michelle were already seated. Keysha put her tray on the table and sat down. Michelle was short and fat but could dress her ass off. Trina was tall and skinny, very pretty but hated being dark skinned.

"What's up?" I said

"Damn, Keysha, are you hungry," Monique said. Keysha was hungry. She had two hamburgers, fries, chips, cookies and a soda.

"Yeah, Monique. I didn't eat breakfast today."

"Your outfit is cute," Michelle said

"Oh, but look at him! Now that's cute," Trina said.

They all looked back to see who it was. There stood Davon Brach.

"I wonder if he has a girlfriend." Trina smiled at everybody.

"Girl, he doesn't want a freshmen, when he is a junior," Michelle told Trina.

"Oh, yes, he does want a freshmen and she's right here at this table," she said. Everyone looked in amazement, wondering who it was he wanted.

"How do you know, Keysha?" Trina said, while turning up her lips.

"He's in my class and he asked me if one of you had a man," she informed them.

"Who?" they all asked.

"It's you, Monique. He gave me his number for you." Keysha smiled, knowing inside she wish it was her. She handed Monique the number. "His name is Davon Brach."

"It must be nice," Trina said.

"Don't hate on Monique. Find your own damn man," Keysha told her. Trina's not going to get an attitude with her cousin.

"Yeah, Trina. We are in high school. There's plenty out there," Michelle let her know.

"I'm not mad. I was just saying," Trina tried to change up.

"Yeah, that's what I thought," Monique finally spoke up.

"So, are you going to call him because if not..." Trina said

"Oh, yes, she is going to call him. So hop off." Keysha looked her dead in the eyes.

The warning bell rang and Keysha grabbed her cookies, put them in her purse and ran off to class. The day was finally over. Keysha caught her bus and as usual it was hot and funky. She sat right in front so she could get off the bus first and run straight for her house. It was Keysha's stop, finally! She poured out of her seat, got off the bus and ran up to her door. She had to take a dump from eating so fast at lunch today. Keysha's rule was no pooping in school. She took her keys out to open the door.

She came through the kitchen and ran for the steps. Keysha went straight for the bathroom to handle her business. After she finished handling her business, she jumped directly in the shower. Now that Keysha was refreshed she wanted to tell her mother about

her day at school. So for some reason, in the midst of excitement, she decided not to knock. That was a big mistake. She busted right in on her and Mr. Jones having sex. Mr. Jones had her bent over the bed doggy style. She looked up at Keysha and didn't even stop.

"Shut the fucking door, Keysha." She yelled at her. Keysha slammed the door and ran to her room. She locked her door and began to get dressed. She sat there and thought to herself, 'My mom is crazy!' 'Enough of thinking about Pamela,' she thought, 'now let Keysha concentrate on Keysha.' She grabbed her book bag and pulled out her homework. Just at that time her mother knocked on the door. Keysha sat there like she didn't hear anything.

"Keysha, open the door."

"I'm doing my homework right now, Mom."

"Open this door." She got up to open the door and Pam came in.

"How was school today?" she asked

"Why were you sleeping with Mr. Jones?

Does Mrs. Jones know what the two of you were doing?"

"First of all, what I do is none of your concern, and yes, she knows." Keysha just sat there looking pissed off.

"Your doctor's appointment is today," she said to Keysha.

"What appointment?" Keysha looked at her.

"To get you on the Pill," she reminded her. Keysha just sat there with this deep feeling in the pit of my stomach.

"We don't have a car."

"Yes, we do. Mr. Jones is letting us use his, so let's go Keysha," she stated

"Right now, Mom?"

"Yes, right now." She looked her in the face. They walked out together to go to the doctors' office.

The Jones' had money. He drove a white Navigator with rims and the whole works. His wife also drove the same type of truck, only black. Mr. Jones was in the military and his wife was a nurse. They pulled up to the

building. Keysha started to feel queasy. Her mom turned to her, so she could prep Keysha before she went into the office.

"Keysha, do not tell the doctors you had sex with James."

"Why not?"

"So neither he nor I will have to go to jail."

"What do I say then?"

"Nothing."

They got out of the car. Pam and Keysha went in and her mom signed her in. They were waiting five minutes before they were called back.

This was the first time Keysha met Dr. Delgatto. She was a small petite Spanish lady with very long, wavy hair.

"Hello, Keysha, how are you today?"

"Fine."

"So this is your first time at the gynecologist's and I want to go over some things with you."

"Okay."

"Mrs. Williams, you can go into the

waiting area."

"No, that's okay," her mom said. She was looking very nervous.

"No, Mrs. Williams. I'm not asking you. I'm telling you. I have private questions to ask my patient." So she rose from the chair slowly and walked out the door.

"Okay Keysha. Why do you want to get on the Pill?" She got right to the point and Keysha was stunned at how she was so blunt.

"Because I don't want to get pregnant," she told her.

"Well, that's smart. Are you having sex?" Keysha felt so embarrassed and then she finally answered her.

"Yes, ma'am."

"Did you use protection?"

"Yes."

"What did you use?"

"A condom."

"Okay. That's good."

Pam was hoping Keysha did not tell the doctor about James. She was feeling a little nervous. Pam looked up and Keysha was

walking towards her with a prescription.

"Mom, are you ready?"

"Yeah, is everything alright?"

"Yeah, everything is good."

They got in the car. Keysha turned the radio up. Her mom reached over and turned it down.

"What did you tell the doctor?"

"Nothing."

"Did she ask you if you were having sex?"

"Yes."

"And what did you tell her."

"I told her I was having sex." She reached over and slapped Keysha upside my head. "Dumb ass.".

"Mom, I didn't tell her who," she cried.

"Thank goodness," she said. "What kind of birth control did she give you?"

"Something called the 'patch'."

"Good, good," she said with this strange look in her eyes. Keysha didn't like it.

"Why is that so good?" she asked her.

"Keysha, James is coming over tonight."

She took a deep breath and looked at her mom. "What does that have to do with me?"

"He is bringing over five hundred dollars tonight," she smiled at her.

"Mom, not tonight please," she begged her to no response.

"Keysha, shit, we need the money."

"Then you sleep with him!" Keysha yelled.

She pulled the car over and punched her in the face. Keysha's nose started to bleed.

"Now I don't know who the fuck you think you talking to, but don't you ever disrespect me again. I run shit here. Not the other way around."

"Why are you starting to hit on me now?" she cried.

"Because you don't listen, and I can do what I want to you," she said. "And don't get any blood in this truck."

Pam turned the music back up and pulled off. Keysha reached in the glove compartment to get a napkin to clean up her face. Once they reached the house, Keysha

jumped out of the car. She went straight to her room. Keysha stretched out across her bed. She decided right then and there that she would make her mom sorry for hitting her. Just then the phone rang and she just let it.

"Keysha, get the phone!" Mom yelled from downstairs.

"Who is it?"

"It's Monique."

"Hello?"

"What's up, Cousin?"

"Nothing."

"What's the matter with you?" Monique questioned her.

"Nothing."

"Okay. Where have you been at all day?"

"At the doctors'."

"For what?"

"I'll tell you in a minute. So what's the big emergency?"

"I called Davon today."

"For real? What did he say?"

"He wants me to hang out with him on Friday."

"I hear that. That's what's up."

"What's going on with you? I can hear it in your voice."

"Everything."

"Is Aunt Pam acting crazy again?"

"Isn't that always the case?"

"Keysha!" Mom yelled.

"Hold on, Monique, my mom's calling me."

"Yes."

"I'm going over to the Jones' to play cards. I'll be back later."

"Okay."

"Monique, I'm back."

"So why did you go to the doctors' today?"

"To get some birth control."

"Birth control?"

"Yeah."

"For what?"

"What do you think?"

"Does Auntie know?"

"Yeah, who do you think took me?"

"Oh. That's why she was tripping."

"Not exactly."

"Are still you a virgin?"

"No."

"When were you going to tell me?"

"I don't know."

"Does Auntie Pam know?"

"Oh, yeah, she knows," she said sarcastically.

"Did she flip out or what?"

"Or what."

"What's the matter?"

"Can I talk to you about something? I don't want anybody to find out about this, especially Aunt Jackie."

"Okay," she agreed.

"You have to promise, Monique."

"I promise."

So Keysha told her the whole story about James. She also told her about the way her mom had been hitting her lately.

"I can't believe it! James? Kesh?" She sounded so shocked.

"Yeah, I know."

"I can't believe Auntie would do that."

"He's coming back tonight."

"What?"

"Yeah, Mommy says we need the money."

"Shit, who needs money that bad? Let her get her big beefy ass up and do it then." They both started to laugh.

"You don't have to do it, Keysha. I'll tell my mom and we can come and get you."

"You promised, Monique."

"He is a rapist, you know."

"Don't start. I'll see you tomorrow at school."

"Keysha, please!"

"I'll be alright. Call your new man."

"Yeah, that's my man! An upper classmen. Love you. Talk to you tomorrow."

"Love you, too." And she hung up the phone.

Once off the phone with her cousin, she got ready because James would be there in a few minutes. Her revenge would begin tonight, starting with James. She got up and put on her mom's see through bra and panties she stole.

She then lit some scented candles and sprayed some sensual perfume. There was a light knock on the door.

"Come in." She tried to not sound nervous but sexy.

"Hey, Keysha," James said with a dirty old man smile on his face.

"What's up?" she smiled at him.

"Oh, yeah, here is two hundred dollars for you." He handed her the money.

"Wait a minute. My mother said five hundred dollars."

"Yes, but I had to give her three hundred." He seemed nervous, thinking he wasn't going to get his new tender pussy.

"Oh, really? I'm doing all the work and I think I'm worth the full amount, don't you?" She said this while grabbing his crotch.

"Oh, yes, you most definitely are." He reached back in his pocket and gave her an extra two hundred dollars. "This is all I have. Is this enough?"

"Yeah, this time. But if I'm doing all the favors, I want all the money." Keysha started

kissing James on his mouth, which he understood was a no-no. He opened her robe and saw the panties and bra. He began to breathe heavy. She backed up and took off the panties, bra and robe.

"Get on your knees and lick my ass, James."

"Damn, you sure have come into yourself since Saturday."

"You're talking when you should be licking." 'It felt good to be in control', she thought. He started pleasing her. She began to moan and leaned her head back. James picked her up and laid her on the bed and started taking off his clothes.

"Wait a minute." I said to him "Let me blow out the candles. She went over blew out the candles and unlocked the door in hopes that her mother would peek in on them.

"Hurry up, I'm about to burst over here!" James begged.

"Here I come, James." She felt like she could call him by his first name. Since he was always over at the house fucking her, calling

him by his first name seemed fair. He pulled her on top of him and started kissing her breasts. Keysha really began to get into having sex. It felt good. She heard a noise and a crackling sound. Keysha looked up and, sure enough, her mother was peeking in on her. Now it was time to put on a show.

"Oh, James, kiss me," she said in a lusty voice.

"Oh, hell yeah, Baby. Anything you want." James kissed her on the mouth.

She knew this would burn her mom up. Next James told Keysha he loved her.

"Shit, you feel so good," he said.

So she whispered in his ears. "Tell me I'm better than she is."

"Baby, you better than Pamela is or could ever be." He was just moaning like crazy. "Keysha for real, let's just cut the middle man out of the picture."

"What do you mean, James?" Keysha played like she was dumb.

"Let's meet and not tell your mother," he said.

She leaned in and whispered in his ear. "Okay."

Then she stuck her tongue in his ear, and he started to bang the hell out of her pussy. It felt great and maybe she would really secretly meet him. She will need some practice if she planned on getting her a senior. Keysha was sure after her mom heard their conversation tonight that he would be gone in the morning. 'But what she doesn't know won't hurt her,' Keysha thought. She looked over at her mom closing the door. James never knew she was there, but Keysha certainly did. James got up and left. Keysha went to take a shower and finish up her homework. Then she went to sleep. When she was getting ready for school her mother came and stood in the doorway.

"James won't be coming around here anymore," she said

"Why not?"

"Because I fucking said so."

"I thought you were good friends."

"Like I said, he won't be returning, and I don't want you to have any contact with him."

"Cool with me." Keysha wanted to laugh. She could see the pain in her eyes and Keysha didn't care. This was a woman who was prostituting her own daughter. She turned around and walked out.

"Mission accomplished." So Keysha stood up and turned around, holding her stomach, laughing.

"So you think you did something, huh?" her mom raised her eyebrows.

Keysha turned around. She was standing there in her room. She never heard the door open.

"Mom, what are you talking about?" she asked.

Keysha was scared to death.

"You sneaky little bitch. You thought you could make me mad? Little do you know I don't have love for nobody. I just fuck 'em and get my money." She started walking towards her with a killer look in her eyes. "And that goes for your ass, too. I couldn't do shit with my life because of you," she told her.

"I didn't ask to be born," Keysha yelled

Pam leaped on her and she began hitting Keysha, punching and kicking her.

"You stupid little bitch, trying to fuck with me? I run this motherfucking show. I'll kill your ass first before I let you disrespect me." She said while pulling her hair out.

"Mommy, stop! I'm sorry!" she cried

"No, Bitch. I'll stop when I get ready. You are not grown yet. You'll fuck anybody I tell you to. Do you understand?" She got off her.

"Yes."

"Yeah, like I fucking thought. My mission accomplished." She looked at her.

Keysha got up and locked her door. Keysha looked in the mirror. She had a black eye, bloody nose, black and blue bruises all over my body. Her clothes were torn and she had bald spots on her head. Keysha then decided not to cross her mother again. She guessed that she would be out a couple of weeks of school.

CHAPTER 4

Keysha had been to hell and back her freshmen year. The year was finally coming to an end. She sat on the bus thinking about all the shit she had endured that year. First being a sex slave to James; even though the money was great she seemed to be losing herself in it all. After all, like her mother said, 'Use your pussy while you can still get money for it.'

"Hey, cuz, tonight's the party and tomorrow afternoon it's off to my dad's."

"I know, girl. I can't wait to go see something new. These nigga's around here are beat."

"My dad has so many plans for us. I can't wait to see him."

"I miss Uncle Gerald too."

Really she didn't miss him, she missed her own father, whoever he was. Keysha fantasized that maybe if she could find him he

would want to take her away from her crazy-ass mother. They could have father and daughter time like Monique and her father did.

"Did you hear me, Keysha?"

"Huh, what?"

"What are you wearing to the party tonight?"

"Something really sexy and really cute."

"You are so nasty!"

"If you were even half as nasty as me maybe you could say you have a man."

"I'm fourteen! What do I need with a man?"

"If you have to ask, you're right. You don't need one. I can't believe Auntie Jackie is letting you go to a senior party. She never lets you do anything."

"Well, she knows Shariece's family and is real tight with her mom. Shit, I still have to be home at ten."

"Damn, Monique, your ass can't do anything." Tion interrupted.

"You would think with forty or more kids on this fucking bus and as loud as they are

we could talk in peace!" Keysha yelled.

Tion was leaning over the seat laughing and acting like a fucking idiot.

"Mind your fucking business, you nosey bitch," Keysha told him.

"What? You Moe's bodyguard now?"

"That's alright Keysha it's not his fault that his mother could give a damn about whether he lives or dies."

"Fuck you."

The bus got very quiet and everyone began looking in their direction, including the bus driver. She didn't say anything to them for once. The driver looked in the mirror, smiled and winked at Monique and Keysha. She could not stand Tion. He would always hit her in the back of the head with paper. One time while on a field trip the bus driver, who is 5'2 and white as a ghost with really curly red hair said, "Okay, sorry to say the air conditioner is broke."

The kids started to act crazy. You know nigga's and heat don't match. The whole ride home she kept complaining about how hot she was. So Tion's dumb-ass dumped cold water

down her back. Keysha had never seen a white woman turn so red. She slammed on the brakes and commenced to cussing that ass out. He felt so stupid with his mixed ass. He claimed he is only black but his mother is white. So that means he is basically white.

"Anyway, back to what I was saying. Auntie plays no games when it comes to you."

"What time do you have to be home?"

"Don't even play! When I get there."

"Are you leaving when I leave or are you staying until the party is shut down."

"Depends on who's there, chica."

"Okay, now you're a Spanish whore."

"Correction: I am a great international ho. Yes! Finally at school."

"You act like you like school."

"I like the last day and shaking my ass at all the parties."

It seemed to Keysha that the day was dragging by so slowly. She watched the clock. It was two fifteen and finally time to go. The teacher stopped us to pass out report cards for the year and everyone rushed to see if they

would go to the next grade. Keysha was next in line to receive her report card. She had missed more than thirty days because of her mom's abuse, but she felt really confident she had passed. Keysha opened it and she had six A's and one B.

"Tenth grade, here I come."

She was so happy to be off that funky yellow bus. Keysha stepped into the house and in the kitchen was a tall all-American white man standing there. Her mom was up to her tricks again.

"Hey, Mom! I got my report card. All A's and one B."

"That's good Keysha. This is Mr. Grimes."

"Hi, how are you? Great work at school. Congratulations."

"Thank you."

Keysha ran upstairs to go to her room. Pam could give a damn about her. All she was concerned with was making that money. She opened her bedroom door to the same old splattered with pink and purple. Keysha

decided that when she come back from Ohio
she was going to change her room. There was a
knock at the door.

"Come in."

It was the white man from downstairs.
Keysha was so scared and he walked right into
the room.

"Can I help you?"

"Yes, your mother told me to give you
this four hundred dollars and you would know
what to do." He was very nervous and even
looked a little scared but not too afraid to come
up here and get this tender pussy.

"She said what? I will be right back."

Keysha tore out of her room. She was
ready for any kind of confrontation that may
happen. She flung the door open.

"Mom, you are not my pimp."

"Keysha, today is not the day. I will fuck
you up."

"Why do I have to fuck him? Why can't you?"

"One, because I told you to and second,
it's that time of the month for me or I would."

"I hate you."

"You can hate me all you want."

She got up and slammed Keysha up against the wall and began to choke her. Keysha was about to black out. She stopped and let her go. Keysha knew not to make her any angrier than she already was.

"Now go take care of Mr. Grimes."

Keysha slowly walked back to her room and there stood Mr. Grimes. This man was the all American white boy type. He had on Dockers, a button down oxford shirt and loafers. He was just a white boy. This made her sick to her stomach.

"Okay, Mr. Grimes, take your clothes off."

"Just like that?"

"Yes, I don't have all day. I have other things I have to do."

He took off all his clothes and he was even whiter than he appeared. Keysha walked towards him. He was already hard. She laid on the bed and spread her legs.

"Wait one minute. I'm nervous and I

need a boost."

"What are you nervous about?"

"I have never been with a black woman before."

"Well, all pussy is pink on the inside."

"Yeah, I guess. I need a pep-up. Are you cool with that?"

"Yeah, it's cool with me, Mr. Grimes."

"Please call me Todd."

Todd reached into his pocket and pulled out some coke. He made two lines on her dresser. He bent down and began to snort it. He leaned his head and enjoyed it.

"Damn, is it that good?"

"When you need to escape, this is the way to do it. You want a hit?"

"I don't know."

"You don't have to."

"Yeah, fuck it."

Keysha snorted two lines and began to feel herself being lifted out of her body. Todd began to have oral sex with her and she forgot

about him being white or any other color. He was kissing her so very passionately, stroking her hair and obviously enjoyed being with a black woman. She loved the feeling of being high. Shit, nothing mattered to her. She was truly numb to all that was going around her and could act like nothing really happened. The sex was finally over and she was ecstatic about it.

"Thanks, Keysha, and keep the powder just in case you need to escape."

"Good looking, Todd."

She was in her room getting ready for the party. She was thinking about how she just had sex with some white man and she felt sick to her stomach. In came her mom, not saying sorry to her at all. Pam wanted to know if Keysha had all her stuff packed to leave.

"What time is your aunt coming to pick you up?"

"At seven in the morning."

"Good, I need a break from you."

Keysha needed a break from her to, but because she feared for her life so much she kept

that thought in her head.

Jackie dropped Monique and Keysha off at the party. Jackie had to walk them in and introduce them to everybody she knew. Keysha and Monique were so embarrassed.

"Your mom is embarrassing."

"You mean your Aunt."

"Yes! She is leaving."

"Auntie is coming over here."

"I will back to pick up both of you at eleven."

"Oh, Auntie I don't have to be home until one."

"Yes, I'm sure you don't. Like I said, I will be back to pick up the both of you at eleven. Be happy I gave you an extra hour. Note to the two of you: don't make me look for you."

Keysha loved her aunt and would never disrespect her. So she would be leaving at eleven o'clock. She needed to rest up for Ohio anyway.

Keysha heard a horn blowing outside. She looked over and her clock was blinking twelve. The power went out last night. She

leapt up and threw her clothes on, ran to brush her teeth and grabbed her bags.

"Bye, Mom! I'm leaving for Ohio."

"Bye, have fun."

"Hi, everybody."

"You just woke up, didn't you?"

"Yes. The electricity went out last night. I didn't know."

They were all rushing to get to the airport and get checked in. They kissed her aunt and ran to the gate to catch their plane. Keysha had never been on a plane before and she was scared as hell. Monique visited her father every summer and holidays, so she was used to flying back and forth to Ohio.

"Are you excited?"

"More like scared as hell."

"Just think about all the fun we are going to have."

"I know. Let's just hope we make it."

"Girl, shut up."

They were finally in Ohio and boy was Keysha glad to get off that plane. The people were knocking her over and babies were crying.

They walked down the long hall to get into the terminal and then went to wait for the luggage. There was Uncle Gerald, looking as handsome as ever. Monique ran to him and gave him a big hug. Keysha's anxiety level was through the roof. She ran to the bathroom, took two snorts and she felt much better.

"Where is she going?"

"I think her stomach is upset. She has never flown before. Oh, here she comes."

"Hey, Keysha, come give me a hug."

"Hi, Uncle Gerald."

"Let's get your bags and head out."

Gerald drove a black Yukon truck and it was big and long. Keysha was so happy not to be in Savannah, Georgia and away from her mom. She could actually have fun and be a kid for once. They pulled up into the driveway and there was a whole bunch of people in the front yard as well as the back yard. Keysha felt a little scared. These were not her people and she knew no one. Keysha got of the car and everyone was hugging Monique and her.

"Look at Moe! All grown up! And is this

Keysha," the unfamiliar voice said.

"Hi, Auntie Linda, this is my favorite cousin, Keysha."

"Hi, honey."

"Hi, Mrs. Linda."

"No, baby, it's Aunt Linda."

"Oh, now that's your favorite cousin."

"Hi, Matt, and I can have more than one favorite cousin."

"Hi, I'm Matt, your competition for favorite cousin."

"Hi, I'm Keysha and I believe I got you beat on that one."

"Oh, you got a little attitude. You are going to fit in great with us."

Monique's family really knows how to party. There was a DJ, so much food they could feed the homeless and a pool. Keysha ate, danced and socialized; something she never really did. The cookout was finally over and they never even made it into the house.

Keysha walked into the house and the first room she came to was the living room. It was beautiful, so clean and not a roach in sight.

The paintings on the wall, the cream colored sectional and beautiful candles everywhere. This is where Keysha got her love of beauty from. Keysha walked around in astonishment. Just ahead was the kitchen. It had granite counter tops, marble floors and a dishwasher.

"Hey, baby, your room is upstairs to the right."

"Thanks, Uncle Gerald. Your house is beautiful."

"You are very welcome here. I love having you here. Get some sleep because tomorrow we are going to the amusement park and shopping."

"Thanks again, Uncle Gerald, for everything."

He gave her a hug and she went upstairs. Keysha went into the room and Monique was already showered and asleep. Monique played no games. She got her rest.

Keysha looked around the room and became instantly jealous. The room looked like it was decorated by a hired designer. There was

two twin beds with matching light blue comforters, beautiful dolls on the matching dresser set she had and every game you could imagine: Monopoly, Sorry! And Uno. She fell down on the bed and was so happy to be there.

The next morning they awoke to the smell of bacon, pancakes and eggs. Keysha was happy to get a hot breakfast. She usually got Honeycombs with milk, if she was lucky. Monique was over in her bed snoring. Keysha loved her cousin so much because she included her in every aspect of her life. Keysha's uncle came in to tell them to get dressed and eat.

"That breakfast was great."

"I'm glad you liked it, Keysha."

"Dad, where are we going today?"

"I am taking my two favorite girls shopping. Tomorrow Matt is taking the both of you to the amusement park because I have to work."

They had been gone since ten o'clock in morning and it was now ten o'clock at night. Gerald bought them shoes, clothes and jewelry.

He did not even give Keysha a limit even though she was not his child. She wished he was her father. This was the best summer ever to her.

* * * * *

The next couple of weeks was filled with the same type of fun. Matt took them to parties and clubs. He was eighteen and they were fifteen, but he did not care. Tonight he was taking them to the movies and dinner because tomorrow would be the girls' last night together.

"Hey, Monique, you ready to go to the movies."

"I don't feel very well."

"What's the matter?"

"I feel like I have to throw up."

"You want me to get Uncle Gerald?

"Yes."

"Okay." She ran downstairs to get her uncle.

"Uncle Gerald, Monique is sick."

"What's wrong?"

"I don't know."

They both went upstairs by that time she was in the bathroom throwing up. Her face looked so grey and Gerald, being the good father that he was, got a cold cloth and put it on her face and carried her to the bedroom. He then helped her get into night clothes and put her to bed.

"Uncle Gerald, I can clean the bathroom up."

"No baby, get ready to go to the movies and dinner with Matt."

"I can't leave her here while she is sick."

"Go ahead, she will be asleep all night. Go have fun."

"Okay."

"Good. There is Matt blowing the horn now. Ignorant-ass. Tell him I said we are not in the country."

Keysha ran to the car and got in and as usual Matt had his music thumping. He looked

so good, but Keysha had to remember that he was her cousin. The fact is he had braids, white teeth, a tight-ass body and he was so fucking intelligent.

"Where is Moe?"

"She's sick."

"It's just you and me tonight."

"Yeah? You okay with that?"

"Yeah."

They pulled off and went to the movies. While in the movies a couple of his friends were there, and of course, the niggas was checking Keysha out.

"What's good, Matt?"

"Not a damn thing."

"Who is this? Your girl."

"No, this is my cousin Keysha."

"Hi, Keysha. My name is Black."

Was he ever black as hell, ugly and even looked like he stank.

"What's up?"

"You from around here?"

"No, I'm from Savannah, Georgia."

"Aw shit! A Georgia peach in the

building."

"Black, cut that shit out. Get up off my cousin."

"Alright."

"Nice meeting you."

"Bye."

"Sorry about that."

"Your friends are ugly." They both laughed.

The movie was so funny; it was *Madea's Family Reunion*. Keysha laughed the whole time she was there. It was finally over and Keysha was a little tired.

"That movie was so funny. I know Moe is going to be mad she missed it, but we can see it again when we get back to Georgia."

"It was funny. Are you hungry?"

"Not really."

"Do you like stars?"

"What?"

"Do you like stars?"

"Yes."

"Good. Do you want to go and see some?"

"Yes. I guess so."

"We are supposed to be able to see meteor showers tonight."

"Oh okay, cool."

So they took off in his car and headed down a dark, curvy road. She was scared, was he going to kill her or shit? She just did not know.

"Why is it so dark and where are we going?"

"I'm driving to this cliff."

"A cliff! Are you going to try and kill me because a bitch can fight?"

"Calm down, patience. It has to be completely dark to see them."

"I knew that."

"Sure you did."

Matt and Keysha pulled up to the cliff and turned off the lights. Matt left the radio on and put down the drop top. There in the sky a star flew by. It was beautiful.

"Make a wish."

"What?"

"When you see a shooting star, you are

supposed to make a wish?"

Keysha closed her eyes and wished he was not her cousin. He was so kind and unlike any other guy she knew. She wanted to make love to him, but that would never happen. He only saw her as his little cousin.

"What did you wish for?"

"I can't tell you or it wont come true."

"So now you believe?"

Matt sat there in silence for hours just watching the stars fall. It was so romantic. The music was playing love songs and Keysha was in heaven. He knew everything about stars and meteors. She was sitting in the car and began to scream.

"What the hell is wrong with you?"

"That's my song!"

"You like Jamie Foxx?"

"Yes. DJ won't you play this girl a love song."

"No, leave the singing to Jamie."

"You are such an ass."

"You want to dance."

"Yeah."

He put his arms around her waist and they danced to the next four songs. Then she looked up at him and they kissed.

"We shouldn't be doing this. You're my cousin."

"No, not really. I am Moe's cousin, not yours," Keysha said.

"I want you."

"I want you, too."

Matt pulled her shirt off and unhooked her bra. He began to suck her breasts. She threw her head back in pleasure. Next he reached under her skirt and pulled down her panties. Keysha was so wet. He looked at her and he knew she also wanted him all along. Matt pulled her skirt up to expose her pussy and began to lick and suck between my legs. She could not let him just turn her out. Keysha pulled him up and unzipped his pants. His pants fell to his ankles. She began to suck him off like her life depended on it.

The more he groaned the hotter she became. He could no longer take it. She got up, lifted up her skirt turned around and bent over

the car to invite him in. He took the invitation.
The sex with him was so great. Keysha believed
if you wished on a star it comes true.

Chapter 5

Pamela was startled out of her sleep by the man snoring in her bed. She looked at a big black man with all his nappy chest hair, ashy elbows and stank ass breath. The disgust in her face was evident but the thirst for money was greater. She pulled back her deep red wine satin sheets and reached over to her oak night stand to retrieve her nightly earnings.

"Damn, only three hundred! Times is hard."

Pam can't believe she fucked this big black funky looking nigga for only three hundred dollars. That's what happened when you pick up a nigga in front of Georgia Regional Mental facility.

This is how she pulled big funky. Pamela was driving down Abercorn Street, and irritated by the heavy two-way traffic, she began to just look at the scenery. The state was popular for its moss hanging from the trees and

the thick smell of magnolia.

The traffic finally began to move when her cell phone vibrated.

"What's good?"

"Mom, when did you start talking like that?"

"Girl, I am just as down as you are. What are you up to?"

"Nothing, I just wanted to let you know that I was fine."

"I had no doubt your uncle was taking great care of you."

"So, what are you doing today?"

"Oh, you know, a little bit of this and that."

"Are you driving and talking at the same time?"

"Yes, let me go. I will talk to you later."

"Aight, one."

"One."

"You sound so funny saying that."

"Whatever. Bye."

Pamela was so excited to not be bothered with Keysha but she kind of missed

the money coming in.

"I hate this Georgia heat. My hair is all sweaty and nasty."

Fifteen minutes later she pulled into a red brick parking lot. Pamela put up the drop top to the apple red Mercedes and turned off the car. She hopped out of the car frontin as if it belonged to her. She hit the alarm and walked toward the building. Pam just knew the whole world was looking at her and she played that role as such. Before she could make her way to the building she noticed a gentleman with Prada glass and Prada dress shoes and her money radar went through the roof. Pamela began to twine her ass back in forth in hopes of getting his attention. What was he doing? Oh, yes, counting money and she was willing to help him count it and take it. As she walked toward him she began to size him up. Pamela walks across the parking lot, his whole physique coming into focus. He was about 5"11, black as hell, bald and he looked a little greasy. His taste in clothes and shoes spoke multitudes about what type of income bracket he was in.

But her question was why was he in front of the building for mental health. Furthermore, what was she doing there?

"Hi, sexy, you look like you are looking for something."

"Oh, yes, I just need some change; all I have is big bills."

"Anything I can help you with?"

"Yes, do you have change for a twenty, so I can get myself a drink on this hot day?"

His breath was kicking; it smelled like he just woke up and came outside, without a second thought of hitting the Colgate, but money was the only thing on her mind. She thought a quick fuck and couple of hundred could be hers.

"I don't but I can get you a drink out of the machine."

"Thank you."

They walked into the building together. She went into her purse, grabbed her wallet and took out a dollar.

"So, what would you like?"

"A Coke, please."

"Not a problem."

"So why is a big strong man like yourself coming here?"

"Oh, I see. You think that I am crazy, huh?"

"No, I didn't say that."

"Well, if you must know. I am in the military.   I just got back from Iraq and they send everyone for an evaluation."

"Oh, okay: to make sure you guys don't blow anything over here."

"Yeah, something like that. So why are you here?"

"Oh, now I'm crazy? My daughter comes here and I am meeting with her counselor to see if she is making any progress. Since her father died, I just don't know what to do with her. She has been so very depressed."

"Sorry to hear that. Is she making any progress?"

"Yes, some, but she has a long way to go. I stand by my baby 100%."

"So I guess having dinner tonight is out of the question?"

"No, that is not out of the question. Fortunately for you my daughter is away on vacation, so I am definitely free. So let me meet with the counselor and we can do that."

Pamela was happy as hell to get some extra easy cash in her pockets. She hoped this motherfucker knew nothing was free. And if he didn't, he would soon. She turned back, looked at him and smiled.

"She is so beautiful and that ass is going to be mine tonight," he said to himself quietly.

Pamela stepped on the elevator and pushed button number seven.

"I hate coming to this place but if I don't I won't get my monthly check," she mumbled to herself as the doors close.

She stepped off the elevator and walked toward the receptionist's desk. The office was so serene and calming. The walls were in an earth tone color and there were pictures of beautiful waves.

"Hi, I have a one o'clock with Dr. Hayes."

"Oh, yes, Ms. Williams. Have a seat and she will be with you in a moment."

She took a seat in the far corner, trying not to be seen. In walked a young Asian woman, very petite with a short pixie haircut. She seemed real scared and unhappy. Pam looked at her thinking, I'm glad I'm not like that.

"Ms. Williams."

Pamela got up and walked with the nurse to Dr. Hayes's office. On the walk to the doctor's office there were positive sayings on the walls. One always touched her heart. Even though she tried not to allow it, it always did. The poem *Journeys Of Life.* The point of the poem was that once people are born, their time begins to tick down to death and they need to make an imprint while on earth. Pamela couldn't bring herself to believe she was deserving of good things.

"Dr. Hayes, how are you today?"

"Great, Pamela, and yourself?"

"Hoping you don't ask me some off-the-wall questions today."

"Why would you say that?"

"I don't know. I just come so I can get my check every month. There is nothing wrong with me."

"So why do you need a check?"

Pamela did not respond. She didn't want to lose her check. Walking over to the plush leather chair, Pamela sat down. Looking the doctor straight in the face hoping it would intimidate her and speed up the session.

"Well, Pam, we left off at your daughter's father and who he might be."

"Did we?"

"Yes. Tell me why you refuse to tell Keysha who her father is or do you even know who it is?"

"Yes, I know who the fuck my daughter's father is. I do fuck a lot, but I use protection. That's why I am still here and not infected with AIDS."

"I told you time and time again not to use that language in my office."

Pamela knew that Dr. Hayes was not playing with her. Dr. Hayes was a black psychiatrist from Brooklyn, New York and did not play.   She was very pretty: 5"11, long brown hair and an hourglass figure. She wore cute professional glasses and a no non-sense attitude toward those who did not care for life.

"Well, no, that was just luck because condoms break. Tell me this.   Doesn't your daughter deserve to decide whether or not to have a relationship with her father? Especially since you know who he is."

"No, the hell... I mean, no she does not. I make the decisions in life."

"You can't keep the truth from her forever. She will ask one day and you will have to tell who he is."

"I'm her father."

"Why are you so scared to be truthful with her? You think she won't love you anymore?"

"No, because knowing who her father is will hurt someone I truly love but can't stand!"

"I don't understand."

"How could you?"

"Just set yourself free and say his name."

"Okay, the father of my daughter is Gerald, my niece's father."

It was silent in the room. The doctor had never had a case quite like this before. It was always craziness with Pam.

"Well, I would have never thought that, but you portray like you hate your sister. You just expressed how much you love your sister."

"Well, I do have some kind of obligation to her. I would never tell her."

"So you can be caring and loving."

"She is my sister, half anyway.   We do have the same mother."

"Why does that bother you? She is still your family."

"You want to know the story why I can't bring myself to have a relationship with her?"

"Yes, it would be a major break-through for you."

* * * * *

Pamela was the only child born to Mary
and Charles Williams. Life with her parents
had been pure hell. Mary was a homemaker
and stood a stout five feet tall, with long black
hair.   Her father was six foot two with big
shoulders and looked damn near white. As long
as she could remember they fought about
everything. Her father was a drunk and his
whole check would go to the local bar. Every
Friday her mother would try to have the house
cleaned up for him. The family stayed in a two-
bedroom box house. They had one couch in the
living room and a T.V with aluminum foil
wrapped on the antenna. In the kitchen there
was a table that leaned to one side and had to
be propped up with anything to even out the
other three legs. Mary did the best with her
limited food supply so she had to get creative
with her meals. Tonight it was fried bologna,
rice and pork'n beans. The door opened and it
was her dad. He reeked of liquor and she knew
that it was over for her mom.

"Hi, Daddy."

"Hey, baby girl."

He put her down and walked over to the stove. The tension in the air was thick and her mother looked very nervous.

"What the fuck is this mess you cooked?"

"Charles, it is all we had. I am doing the best that I can." He slapped her.

"Don't do this, Charles. Not tonight."

"Don't do what?" He picked her up and threw her back down on the floor.

Pamela began to cry and scream. She did not want her dad to beat up her mother.

"Pam go in your room while Daddy talks to Mommy."

She walked to her room but never went in. She hid by the doorway and watched. Her dad walked towards her mother.   She was pleading with him not to hit her.

"Charles, please don't hit me."

"Charles, please don't hit me," he mocked her.

"I do the best I can with the little bit of stamps I get. I can't get a job because Pam is only four years old and we can't afford a babysitter."

"Well, your best isn't good enough."

"Charles, if you would bring some of your paycheck home we could have a little more than what we have now."

"Bitch, who the fuck do you think you are talking to? I don't do enough for this family?"

"I didn't mean..."

"Did I tell you to talk?"

Mary knew to shut up because she knew regardless, she was going to get her ass whipped tonight. She just wanted to make it as painless as possible.

"I can do what I want with my money, do you understand? Do you fucking understand me? Now your bitch-ass can talk."

"Yes, Charles."

"What?"

"Yes sir, Charles."

"Better. Now take off your clothes."

"For what?"

"You questioning me?"

"No sir."

She began to take her clothes off, not sure what he was going to do to her. She stood their butt-ass naked. She glimpsed over at the door and saw Pam hiding. She wanted to tell her to go in her room but was scared to. She was not allowed to speak.

"Now you want to tell Charles what to do, right?"

Charles began to take off his thick leather belt. He wrapped the strap around his hand with just the buckle hanging.

"Charles, please don't hit me!"

He reached his hand back and swung forward with all his might. He struck her mother and she fell and began to scream.

"Mary, get your ass up and put your hands on the chair and don't move! If you do I am going to fuck you up for real!"

She got up, her back stinging from the first blow. Pamela's mom put both her hands on the chair and stood there.

"Do not speak and don't move or I will kill you."

He continued to hit her and hit her. She stood there not moving, tears ran down her face. It seemed like forever that he beat her.

"You can move now."

She could barely move. She went to grab her clothes and put them on.

"Leave those clothes there; come and get on your knees and take care of me."

She knew that meant suck his dick until he came in her face. He loved to degrade her and keep her under his control.

"Charles, please. Pam..."

"Mary, my arms are not tired. Do you want some more? Pam is in her room and she knows to stay there. You say one more word and I'm going to hurt you."

She walked over towards her husband and glanced over at her daughter. She did not want her to see this. As Charles pulled his pants down he noticed Pam. He smiled and told Mary to hurry up. She knelt down and began performing oral sex on him. Sickened at the

fact that her daughter was watching, she threw up. He went into frenzy and began to punch and kick her.

"Oh! My dick ain't good enough for you to suck?"

"Charles, please! Pam is by the door."

"Pam, get in here!"

"Charles, no. Don't!"

Pam came in the kitchen. Her heart was pounding. She did not know what was going on but her dad was hurting her mommy.

"Since you want to see what big people do, sit you ass over in that chair over there."

Her dad had never talked to her in that tone before. She was terrified.

"Mary, lay your ass on the table and open up your legs."

"Pam, go in your room."

"I told her to sit her ass right there. Now get your ass on the table like I said."

"Charles, in front of your daughter?"

"Mary, get on the fucking table now! I want some pussy and yours belongs to me."

"I can't do that in front of her."

"I tell you what: Either you get up here or Pam does."

Mary could not believe he would even contemplate raping his own daughter. She got on the table and laid back.

"Just what I thought. Pam, what I am about to do is what all women do for their man, and one day you will have to do it for you husband. If you get one, don't be a dumb bitch like your mom."

He opened her legs and she began to shake with fear. He took his fingers and stuck them inside her.

"Damn, your pussy is dry and tired. You need to get that bitch wet because I am not trying to burn myself fucking you."

He got up and went to the cabinet and got the cooking oil. He opened her legs and poured it all over her.

"Yeah, because Daddy likes a juicy pussy."

He pulled her to the end of the table and turned her on her stomach. He put his dick inside her and began moving back and forth.

Pam just looked at her dad. Not knowing what he was doing, she began to cry.

"Pam, baby, it is going to be alright."

"Go to your room and stay there this time!"

She got off the chair and ran to her room, not to return to hide outside the door again. She could hear her dad screaming and she didn't know why. She shut her door and went to bed. Mary came in the room to check on her daughter, who was already asleep.

"I promise, baby, it will get better," she whispered to her.

The next day would be the last day she would see her father. He said he was going to the bar and he never came back. She overheard her mom on the phone talking to one of her friends, saying he could not forgive himself for how he made Pamela watch, and she would be better off without him.

Chapter 6

It had been two years since Pam had seen her dad. Mary was dating a man named Kevin Jones and he wanted to marry her. She would never be married again and they just planned to live together. Kevin was a little taller than Mary and had gorgeous honey brown skin and a beautiful attitude. She met him while she attended college. He was a professor there and encouraged her to pursue her dream of becoming a social worker to help other battered women. He was also very kind to Pamela .He took the whole family out, not just Mary. She made it very clear that she was a package deal.

"Pamela, come her."

Mary and Kevin were sitting on the new patio furniture they had just gotten to go with the swing-set in the backyard. Mary looked so happy she was glowing.

"Yes, Mom."

"I know that you are only six but I need to tell you something."

She didn't know what they wanted to tell her but she could tell it was serious. Her mom and Mr. Kevin were holding hands.

"I'm a big girl."

"We know."

"Well, Mommy and Mr. Kevin are going to have a baby."

Pam just looked at them. She really did not know what it meant but she knew she would have somebody to play with.

"Yeah! I'm going to have a little sister!"

"Well, we don't know if it is a girl or boy yet. Are you okay with this?"

"Yes, now I have someone to play with." She skipped back to her swing-set.

"That went well."

"Yes, it did."

Later that year Jackie was born and everything seemed to be going very well with the family. Pamela did everything for her sister. She liked pretending to be the mommy.

Several years passed by and Pam was a
teenager and Jackie a pre-teen and the troubles
began.

She began to realize that her parents
treated Jackie better than her. Pam wanted a
car because she had just turned sixteen. She
had just come out of the DMV.

"So, Mom, when can I get a new car?"

"Pam, as soon as you save half the
money, Kevin and I will pay the other half."

"Good thing for me! All that working
this summer paid off and I have fifteen
hundred saved up."

"Okay, Pam, let's talk to your dad when
we get home."

On the way home she could only think
about what kind of car she would get. Pam had
worked all summer at McDonald's. She saved
all her checks, not even spending one dime.
She wanted to go to school this year in a nice
ride. They pulled up in to the drive-way of the
bi-level house. The lawn was landscaped with
flowers everywhere.

As they parked her sister and dad were in the swing on the porch smiling. Jackie ran up to the car.

"Did you get your L's?"

"And you know this, man!"

"Yeah, girl, I can go to the mall all the time now."

"We."

"Yeah, we, right."

Pam got out of the big black shiny SUV and walked over to the porch where her mom and dad were swinging.

"Dad, I got them."

"That's great, baby girl."

"So when can we go car shopping? I want to begin school in style."

"You have money for a car?"

"Yes, I have fifteen hundred saved up." She was so proud of herself

"You still have to by clothes for school and you have to get your school supplies."

She could not believe this! He was going back on his word. Her mother just looked at

him but did not question him.

"You said if I saved my money for half you guys would pay the other half."

"Did we? I don't remember."

"Mom remembers."

"Pam just don't worry about it. You will get your car; just keep saving."

She could not believe her mom would take up for him like that. They both said it and now she had to get all her stuff by herself.

"So you are just going to take up for him even though he is lying?"

Kevin jumped up and slapped her dead in the face. Her mom sat there and looked at the floor. Jackie leapt on his back.

"Get off my sister!"

He turned around and put her in a bear hug.

"Baby, stop! Don't hit your father."

"Why are you hitting my sister?"

"Your sister is disrespectful towards me and I am not going to take it. Your mother and I pay the bills here, not you. You will do what I say. I'm saying right now, apologize to me."

Pam stared at that fool like he was crazy. She'd be damned if she apologized to him.

"Apologize for what? It is true. You are a liar."

He tries to slap her again and her mother finally got in the way.

"Kevin, what are you doing?"

"She is not going to talk to me like that. Hell, she is not even my daughter but I take care of her like she is mine. She will not disrespect me!"

"Well you took on that responsibility when you got involved with me."

"I have one daughter and that is the only one I will be taking care of. If she wants anything she should ask her trifling-ass father."

"I will, you bastard."

Why did she say that? That was the straw that broke the camel's back.

"That's it! When I come back, I want her gone."

"What are you talking about?"

"Mary, I can't take her anymore. It is either her or me."

He jumped in his car and pulled off.
Kevin was gone about a week when he called
her mother on the phone.

"Hello."

"Hi, baby. I miss you."

"I miss you, too. When are you coming
home?"

"Did you contact Pam's father?"

Her mom took the receiver from her ear
and looked at it.

"Are you serious? You won't come back
unless she is gone?"

"I meant what I said. I won't deal with
her. I will take Jackie and we can get a place
together. You and Pam can get a place."

"I can't believe you want me to choose
between my daughter and you."

"Mary, I love you, but I can't do it
anymore."

Mary realized he was not playing and
her desire to have a family would win out over
her motherly responsibility to her child.

"I will get everything ready."

"Okay, baby, I will be over to get Jackie."

Pamela was hiding behind the door and began to cry. She knew she would be leaving the only family she had ever known to stay with a man she barely knew.

* * * * *

"So, Dr. Hayes. That's why I don't have a relationship with my sister."

"That would not be your sister's fault."

"She got everything and I went to live with a man who set me on the path to prostitution and drugs and nobody ever helped me."

"That still is not you sister's fault. Put the blame on the person who deserves it: your father and mother."

"Well, my mother and Kevin died in a plane accident two years later and Jackie went to go stay with her grandmother."

"What about your dad?"

"What about the motherfucker? He is in jail where he belongs. I don't want to talk

anymore. The hour is up."

"Next week, same time."

"Yeah, whatever."

As she took the elevator back down She was hoping her new meal ticket would be waiting and he was.

"Is everything okay with your daughter?"

"As well as to be expected. Let's go have some fun."

"I'm down with that."

CHAPTER 7

It was a great summer vacation. Keysha got a new car and she went to Hawaii with her mom and her mom's new friend Colin. It was the start of her senior year. Monique and Keysha had plans to go to the mall to do some shopping. Keysha gave her a call to see if everything was still a go.

"Hello."

"Hey, Keysha."

"What's wrong with you?"

"I don't feel good today."

"Do you still want to go shopping?"

"Girl! Hell yeah!"

"Okay. Well, I'll be there in an hour."

Once Keysha hung up the phone she went straight to her closet to change her clothes and headed out to the car. On her way to Monique's house she stopped by Burger King and picked up our favorite meal.

Beep....Beep.

"Come on, Monique, damn!" she yelled. Monique came to the door and put one finger up indicating that she was coming. She ran over to the car.

"Damn, Keysha, I was coming. The mall's not going to run out of clothes, you know."

"You look like shit."

"Thank you."

"Anyway, I brought you some lunch."

"No, thank you. My stomach is upset."

"Damn, shitty ass."

"Whatever. We all have to poop. I got some scoop for you." She grinned. "I had sex with Lamar while you were gone this summer."

"What? When? How?"

"Slow down. The when was at his college graduation party. The how, I think you know that one."

"Wait a minute. At the party? I was still there." I gave her a 'You're just now telling me look?'

"Well, you know." She smiled. "In an,

I'm sorry kind of way."

"No, bitch, I don't. You know we tell each other everything."

"Sorry, you're right. I should have told you but you're all busy with your boyfriend, Tyrese."

"Never too busy for you." I grabbed her hand. "Well, have you done it since?"

"First, let's pull out of the driveway before my mom think something is wrong with us."

Keysha pulled out of the driveway and drove towards the mall. She turned to her at a red light, for her to continue.

"Well we've been having sex damn near every night since the party."

"Was you scared to do it?" Keysha asked.

"Yeah, a little, but to be honest, I was so horny. I thought it was about time."

"I would say so, too. Since you and Davon have been together for four years and you haven't given him any."

"I think he was getting tired of me taking forever and I was tired of being the good

girl all the time."

"So does he have a big dick?"

"I really don't have anyone to compare him to."

"Girl, you know his dick is big regardless." I had to slam on brakes. This old lady was trying to get this front parking spot. "No, you don't old bitch. This is my spot, so get to moving." The old lady just rolled her eyes at her. Keysha hurried and pulled into the parking space.

"Girl, she was about to take her cane out the trunk and do some damage on your ass." Monique laughed.

"Yeah, I don't discriminate. I'll whip an old person's ass too."

"Your ass is going to jail."

"Yeah, right. Now back to the big dick."

"Enough about big dicks. Let's go shopping."

They went into the mall. They were in there for five hours. Keysha and Monique went to the Parisan, Rave's and Petite Sophisticates.

Keysha bought a pair of Gucci boots and some lingerie from Victoria's Secret. Oddly, Monique bought nothing. She was in deep thought. Keysha thought they had been there long enough. She also had to unpack her stuff from her vacation. She had been home for one day and she hadn't put anything up.

"Monique are you going home or coming over to my house," Keysha asked her. Then she burst into tears.

"What's the matter?"

"I need to tell you something else about Davon and me."

Keysha started to feel a little concerned because Monique never really got upset. Or did she keep secrets from her? Keysha usually kept them from her. But she didn't tell her about sleeping with Davon.

"Tell me what."

"You have to promise not to tell anyone."

"Moe, what's going on? You know I always keep our conversations only to me."

"Okay, I think I am pregnant."

"With what?" she said. She really didn't believe her. She always preached about college and not having kids until she was financially set.

"Keysha, stop playing. I'm serious." She began to cry.

"Well, are you sure? Did you take a pregnancy test?"

"No. But my period was supposed to come on two weeks ago."

"Didn't you use protection?"

"No."

"Why not?"

"I don't know why, Keysha!"

"Well, damn." Keysha just looked at her. "Let's go to the pharmacy and get a pregnancy test to be sure."

"Where will I take it at?"

"My house."

"What about Aunt Pamela?"

"She's gone for the night with her new man. She won't be back until tomorrow."

"Okay, I'll call my mom and tell her I'm

staying at your house tonight."

Monique was on the phone with her mom. Keysha was secretly glad it wasn't her that may be pregnant. She could not believe it! Wholesome Monique? And everyone said it would definitely be her. Keysha pulled out of the parking space and headed to the pharmacy.

"Okay, my mom went for it," Monique smiled.

"Good. Okay, let's go get the test to see for sure."

They pulled up to the Rite-Aid, got out of the car and went into the store. Monique started to get nervous. She was looking left and right like she was about to steal something.

"What the hell are you doing?" Keysha asked her.

"I don't want anybody to see me."

"You should have thought about that before you went and got buck wild. Anyway, fuck those people. They don't know you." If there were any people in herewith us. It was just Monique, the cashier, the pharmacist and Keysha.

"Keysha, don't start."

"I'm just saying. They don't know you, fuck'em."

"Yeah, you are right."

So they finally got the pregnancy test, went to the counter to pay for it and there stood an old wrinkled white lady with her nose in the air. What is it about these old people today? So she took the box looked at it and shook her head.

"What the fuck you shaking your head at!" she said.

"Well, such a fowl mouth! You can't be no more than sixteen years old." She scowled at them.

"I'm not here for you to guess my age but to ring up my shit," Keysha told her. She rang up the test and threw Keysha's change on the counter.

"I hope you're not pregnant, the way you behave," the old lady said to her.

"Watch your back when you get off work, you old bitch," she yelled on her way out

of the store. While riding in the car they laughed so hard at the old lady in the store.

"That old wench," Monique said.

"You mean nosey old bitch. Like she has to take care of somebody's baby?"

"Yeah, that too." Monique was still laughing.

Keysha pulled back up in the parking lot and was happy to see her house. Monique got out with a very sad look on her face. Keysha put her arms around her and told her it would be all right. They got in the house and Keysha checked to make sure no one was in the house. She gave her the test and Monique went into the bathroom. Keysha headed over to her room just as her cell phone rang.

"Speak to me," she said.

"Hey, sexy," the familiar voice said.

"Hi, James. How are you?"

"Fine. Is your mother around? I don't want her to kill me."

"James, we have been fucking for three and a half years now."

"Yeah, but your mother doesn't know

that."

"Yeah, let's keep it that way."

"I called because I want to see you tonight."

"I don't know. How much money are you talking about? And what do you want to do tonight, because I'm pressed for time today."

"I have a thousand and I want the works."

"The works? What's that?" she asked. She really didn't care because she just dropped a thousand today at the mall. She needed to make that up. Her job at Rave's just wasn't cutting it. That's why this side job of selling this ass sometimes came in handy. Yeah, sometimes she hated doing it but it helps her get anything she desires.

"I want you to come over here with a raincoat on with nothing underneath. I want you to piss all over me and I want you to beat me like I was a bad boy." He started breathing hard.

"You sure do come up with some strange shit. You want me to come in a raincoat and it's not even raining, plus it's like eighty degrees outside. And now you want me to pee on you and beat you. Yeah, I'll do it. It's your money, "she laughed.

"Come around ten o'clock," he said to her.

"I'll be there when I get there. It's my pussy."

"Yeah, but I'm paying for it."

"I'll be there tonight. Right now I have to go." I hung up the phone.

Keysha stretched out on the bed and noticed Monique standing in the doorway with tears and fear in her eyes. She already knew the results of the test.

"What?" Keysha said to her.

"I'm pregnant Keysha." She showed her the test. They both stood in the doorway staring at it.

"What am I going to do? Shit, Keysha it's our senior year and my mom's going to kill

me!" She paced back and forth.

"We will figure it out," Keysha said as she reached to comfort her

"Oh my! Damn Davon." She put her hands over her mouth.

"You didn't tell him you might be pregnant?"

"Actually, I did, but now I have to tell him yes, I am and tell my mom."

"Well, Monique it's not like you have to keep it." She looked at Keysha like she was a stone cold nut.

"Oh, yes I do. That's not an option for me. I wanted to be grown, so I guess I'll have to grow up."

"Well, it's your decision and I'll be here no matter what you decide." She kissed her on the cheek.

"Can I use the phone to call Davon?" she asked

"You don't have to ask to use the phone. I'll be downstairs if you need me." I shut the door behind me and went downstairs.

Once Keysha got downstairs, she jumped on the sofa and turned on the TV. Then her cell phone rang again.

"Aww shit I hope it's not James again. Damn I'm coming give my pussy a break," she said to herself as she picked up her phone.

"What's good?"

"You, baby," Tyrese said.

"Hey, baby. What's good with you?"

"Trying to see you tonight. You've been gone for three weeks and I miss you."

"You miss me or this platinum pussy?"

"I missed you. The pussy is just a bonus."

"I hear that."

"So are you going to come over tonight?"

"Around what time?"

"Ten o'clock."

"It will have to be late night. Monique's over and she's going through some things right now, but I'll come over as soon as I can and stay all night." She was lying. She had to make her money tonight.

Tell Monique she is lucky that I'm willing to share you."

"Thank you for not being upset."

"I'll see you tomorrow and I love you."

"I love you, too."

* * * * *

Someone tapped her on the shoulder and gave her a goofy smile.

"Why did you tell Tyrese you were basically babysitting me?"

"Because I have some other business to take care of tonight."

"Girl, Tyrese is a good man."

"I know. Let's talk about something else."

"I called Davon and he is on his way over here."

"That's good."

"Is it okay if he comes over?"

"Girl, yeah, of course. I have something

to do tonight anyway."

"Not James!"

"Yes, I have to make my money and I don't need you to judge me."

"How can I judge anybody?" She rubbed her stomach. She sat down beside Keysha and put her head in her lap. "We are going to tell my mom tomorrow."

"You sure you want to do that so soon?"

"The sooner the better." There was a knock at the door.

"Who is it?" Keysha asked.

"It's Davon."

Keysha opened the door and let him in. He looked like a scared animal but he should have been scared of her Uncle Gerald.

"Come in. Monique's in the family room," she told him.

"Thank you, Keysha."

"For what?"

"For being there for Monique."

"That's my cousin, and I love her."

He went in the family room and they hugged each other. Monique began to cry.

"Baby, let's go for a ride," Davon said.

"Okay."

"Take your time. Here, take the extra house keys," she told her. Davon and Monique left and Keysha took a shower to get ready for James.

Keysha was sitting in the car with her ass is sticking to this raincoat. It was irritating her, but she had to make her money. She started her car up and left. It was not long before she reached James's house. It was a beautiful penthouse condo. He worked as a sports medicine doctor for a famous football team. No wonder he always had lots of money. Keysha was definitely willing to take it. She started to knock but remembered she had a key. She turned the knob and went in.

His house was lit with lots of scented candles. She looked around and noticed a trail of roses leading to James's room. She followed the trail and entered the room. There was James lying butt-ass naked on his chocolate brown silk sheets. For him to be in his forties he had a banging ass body.

Keysha looked at him and she started to play the role that he always wanted. James liked it when she dominated him but this pissing thing was new to her.

"Get your ass over here and kiss my feet," she demanded of him.

"Yes, Keysha."

"Did I tell your ass to speak?" He didn't say anything else. He just came over and began licking her pumps. He opened up her raincoat.

"What are you doing?" She looked him in the face.

"I want to see your body. I'm begging you. Please, can I touch you?"

"Well, since you're begging, I guess so." He started touching her breasts and putting his finger inside her.

"May I speak?"

"Yes, you may."

"I want to do something different this time, Keysha."

"Like what, James?"

"I want you to do everything I tell you

to."

Keysha was a little hesitant about letting him control anything concerning her, but she wanted that money.

"Okay. We can try it."

"First, I want you to take off your raincoat."

She took off her raincoat and stood there naked. She bent down to take off her shoes, but he stopped her.

"No, leave the shoes on. Go over and lay on the bed with your back against the headboard." So she did.

"Now I want you to finger yourself until you cum." She started finger fucking herself. Keysha started to moan and finally she came. She looked up and James was sitting on the end of the bed rubbing his penis. He seemed like he really enjoyed looking at her.

"James. I just came. Now what do you want me to do."

"Stick your fingers in my mouth." She leaned forward and he began to suck her fingers. This man is a freak. She didn't care as

long as he paid her.

He licked her fingers, under her nails and between her fingers. He wanted to make sure he got all that pussy juice.

"Damn, James, there's nothing else on my fingers but my nail polish."

"Stand up, Keysha." He lied down on the floor.

"What are you doing now?"

"Sit on my face and put your coochie on my mouth."

"Hey, I have no problem having my ass ate."

"I'm not going to eat you out. I want you to pee in my mouth."

"You were serious about that?" She didn't really care as long as he didn't pee on her.

"Yeah, are you going to do it for me?"

"I can, but why do you want me to do that?"

"Does it matter why as long as I'm paying you? You should satisfy my every fantasy."

"You're right. It's your money."

"Make sure you do it slow, so I can savor the moment."

So she sat down on his face and Keysha peed in his mouth. He just laid there and sucked it up like he was drinking through a straw. Next he pushed her up and motioned for me to piss on his chest. This nigga actually came from her peeing on him!

"Thanks, Keysha," he said as he handed her the money.

"For what? We didn't even have sex. All I did was piss all over you."

"That's what I wanted you to do."

"Well, can I take a shower before I leave?"

"Yeah, you know where everything is."

* * * * *

She got into her car horny as hell. She didn't even really get her rocks off. Keysha needed to come tonight. She called Tyrese.

"Hey, baby, I changed my mind."

"Where are you?"

"At the front door," she giggled

"Well, use the key and come in."

"I'll be right in."

She rushed into the house and went straight for his bedroom. She needed him tonight to satisfy her urges.

"What do you have under that raincoat?"

"Everything that you like."

"Well, come over here and get in the bed and give it to me."

She jumped on top of him and began to kiss him and rub his dick. He ripped open the raincoat and began to suck her breasts.

"Damn, Keysha. It seems like you missed me as much as I missed you."

"Yes I did. Now fuck me." And he did just that.

Afterwards she lay in bed thinking that this is the only man she would have sex with for free. Tyrese Johnson was 6'4", with caramel skin, a beautiful smile, and no children. This man was so meticulous, well-educated and so loving. They have been

together for over a year now.
He doesn't know about Keysha's other job.
He loves her for her at least the person he
thinks she is. She met him at a football game
when she was out with James one day. He
thinks James is her dad. Tyrese runs a youth
center for under -privileged children. Tyrese is
older than she is. He is only twenty-one and
Keysha is seventeen. She got out of the bed to
return home. Her mother always told her not to
let the sun beat her home. She kissed Tyrese
and left to go home.

"I'll see you tomorrow?" he said

"Maybe. Love you."

"I love you, too." He turned over and
went back to sleep.

She tip-toed into the house, but her
mom was not home yet. She went to her room
to get her towel to take a shower. There was
Monique in her bed asleep. She grabbed her
towel and went to take a bath. After washing
her night down the drain, Keysha got in bed
with her cousin and went to sleep.

* * * * *

"Hello, girls." her mother said.

"Hi, Mom."

"Hi, Aunt Pam."

"It's one o'clock in the afternoon. Do y'all have plans on getting up today?"

"Yes, right now." She said

"Well, breakfast or lunch is downstairs, and I'm going to get my nails done."

We got up, got dressed and went downstairs to eat. Once in the kitchen there were pancakes, sausages, eggs and fruit on the table. Monique just looked and held her stomach.

"Nothing for me."

"Morning sickness?" Keysha said

"Try all day sickness." She smiled.

"So what are you doing today?"

"Hoping you will come with Davon and me to tell my mom."

"What?"

"Please, Keysha, I need you."

"Alright, but if Auntie gets to beating

ass, my ass is outta of there."

They were about five minutes away from her aunt's house. Monique grabbed Keysha's hand. She looked in her rear view mirror to see Davon with his head in his hands. Keysha knew she never want to go through this. They pulled up and got out of the car.

"Well, baby, you ready?" Davon reached for Monique's hand.

"As ready as I'll ever be." They walked in the house with Keysha following behind them.

"Good morning, peoples," Keysha's aunt said to all of them. Monique broke down crying.

"What's the matter, Monique?" Her aunt said. But Monique couldn't speak.

"Mrs. Williams, could you please sit down?" Davon suggested.

"No, I don't think so, if it's that bad, tell me now."

"Auntie, please sit down." Keysha begged her.

"Okay, what is it?" It got silent for a minute.

"Mom, I'm pregnant."

You better mean pregnant with possibilities."

"No, ma'am. Monique and I are having a baby."

"Don't 'No, ma'am' me. You're just kids yourself and Monique, you're still in high school. I know Mr. Brach here has just finished his two-year degree, but what about you?"

"Mom, I'm still going to college."

"How, Monique? Kids cost money!"

"Mom, I can do it."

"I can help, Mrs. Williams."

I think you've helped yourself enough." She stared him dead in the face.

"Mrs. Williams I just graduated. I have a great job and I will watch our baby while Monique attends college. I'm prepared to take care of my responsibility. I want our child to have to educated parents."

"You know what? I don't need this shit right now, and by the way, call your father."

"Mom, wait!"

Her aunt got in her car and left. Monique started crying again. The whole house was in an uproar. Keysha hugged Davon and kissed her cousin.

"Call me if you need me," Keysha told her

"I will, Keysha, thanks."

Keysha shut the door and drove home. She could not believe the day she had just had. Well, the one Monique was having. Keysha was wondering if she should tell her mother or let her figure it out on her own. She put the key in the door and turned the knob. Keysha walked in and heard some funny sounding noises.

She walked into the family room to see Mrs. Jones' face in the middle of her mother's pussy. She just went upstairs. They didn't even notice her anyway. Thirty minutes later her mother opened the bedroom door.

"Keysha, I need to talk to you."

"About what?"

"About this!" She held up the pregnancy test Monique had thrown in the trashcan.

"What? Are you snooping now?"

"What? Do you want to get punched in your face now? Don't play with me! Are you pregnant?"

"No."

Well, according to this test, somebody is."

"It's not me."

"Well, who then? Because I am about to whip your ass." Keysha just looked at her and motioned her eyes at Monique's picture on her desk.

"Not Monique," she said

"Yes, Mom. Monique is pregnant."

"Did she tell Jackie?"

"That's where I just came from."

"Well, how did she take it?"

"Not so good. She just up and left." Her mom started laughing.

"That's what her better-than-thou ass gets."

"Mom, not today."

"I know. I know. You love your aunt."

"Just like Monique loves you."

"I love her, too, but she has ruined her life. Don't be like that. I'm letting you know right now. I will put your ass out, and I'm not anyone's babysitter."

"Mom, please."

"Okay. I need you to go over to Mrs. Jones' house to get some flour."

Keysha sucked her teeth.

"Do you want to eat tonight?" her mother said to her.

She got up to go next door. Keysha began to think maybe she didn't need to eat tonight.   She just saw this woman eating her mom's ass. She rang the doorbell and Mrs. Jones told her to come in.

"Mrs. Jones, my mom sent me over to get some flour."

"I know, baby, it's in the cupboard." She stared at her sexually.

"Mrs. Jones, why are you looking at me like that?" she asked her.

"Like what?"

"Like the way you look at my mom. I don't see how another woman can please you

the way a man can."

"Do you want a sample?" She smiled.

"No disrespect. But I like a strong, hardy dick," Keysha said in a firm voice.

Mrs. Jones went over to her wallet and pulled out two hundred dollars.

"What is this?"

"Let me taste you, Keysha," she begged.

"I don't go that way Mrs. Jones," she told her. "I don't think so."

Just then Keysha looked down at her arm and saw her diamond tennis bracelet. She noticed Keysha admiring it.

"You want it? Let me taste your pussy."

Keysha took her shorts and panties off. All she could think of was a quick two hundred dollars and a diamond bracelet just for having oral sex. That was cool with Keysha.

"Lie down on the table, Keysha and open your legs." She grinned and then went over to the refrigerator. She got some strawberry quick and poured it on her clit. She bent down and started licking the hell out of her pussy. She threw her head back and began to moan.

"This beats a hard dick, huh?" she looked up from between Keysha's legs.

"Get back down there and finish what you started."

Keysha never had a man eat her the way she did. No wonder her mother saw Mrs. Jones three times a week. Suddenly there was a deep voice in the corner of the kitchen.

"Excuse me," he said

Keysha jumped off the table and grabbed her stuff. Mrs. Jones went over to her husband and kissed him. He licked his lips.

"Tastes good," Mr. Jones said.

Keysha was shocked. She just knew he was going to kill both of them. Mr. Jones was a 5'10" red bone and very, very muscular.

"I didn't mean to interrupt you two. Go ahead and carry on," he said in a deep, husky voice.

So she got back on the table. Keysha was a little apprehensive about it. She had paid for a service not yet rendered.

"Get on all fours," Mrs. Jones commanded.

She continued to lick her. Now she was licking her ass. She looked out the corner of her eye and saw Mr. Jones was naked, rubbing himself.

"Can I join the party?" he asked.

They both looked at her. "Why not?" she said to the both of them. Mr. Jones walked over to his wife and took off her clothes.

"Get off the table," he told her.

Mrs. Jones lay down on the table and he began to perform oral sex on her.

"Keysha, sit on my wife's face." He smiled. "I don't want you to feel left out."

She climbed on the table and sat on her face. She stuck her tongue in her coochie. Keysha felt like going crazy. Next thing she knew, she was on the bottom and Mr. Jones was licking her pussy while Mrs. Jones licked his asshole. He started to go crazy. He jumped up, bent her over the sink and started to fuck her vigorously.

"Keysha, take the money and bracelet on the counter," she said while moaning. "Don't forget the flour."

Keysha put her clothes on and grab the stuff off the counter. She was curious but she couldn't have watched if she wanted to. Keysha had already been gone for an hour and a half. She turned to leave. Keysha looked back to see Mrs. Jones with a strap on dildo fucking Mr. Jones in the ass. And he was taking it like a pro.

"These people are freaks," she said to herself. "Here, Mom. Here is the flour you asked for."

"Took you long enough." She started laughing. "That women can eat a mean pussy can't she."

Keysha just looked at her.

"I told you. Don't knock it until you try it."

CHAPTER 8

This was the last week of high school for Keysha. The year had been a roller coaster ride for both Monique and Keysha. Monique found out that she was one credit short of graduating from school and was due in three weeks.

"Keysha, I don't think I'm going to graduate from school."

"Don't worry. Talk to Mr. Johnson about it."

"I did. He told me that I shouldn't have gotten pregnant."

"What the hell does that have to do with school?"

"I missed a lot of days because I was sick."

"I'm going to talk to his ass."

"No, Keysha. You might make it worst."

"Let me just see what I can do. Okay?"

"Whatever. I can't believe I'm not going

to graduate."

"Oh, yes, you are."

"That's easy for you to say. You're graduating and with honors."

"I don't care. I'm not going to college."

"You should re-think that." She smiled and walked down the hallway to talk to her counselor.

Keysha couldn't let her cousin go to summer school. Who knew if she would ever finish? The baby would be here soon. She walked to the principal's office.

"Hi, Mrs. Brown. Can I speak to Mr. Johnson, please?"

"What's the problem, Keysha?"

"I need to talk to him about graduation."

"Well, can I help you with it? "

"No, I really need to talk to him."

"Well, he's not in right now. Can you meet him after school?"

"Yes, Mrs. Brown. That will be fine."

Since this is the last week of school for seniors, Keysha didn't have a class. She was just finishing up loose ends. She had to make

sure they had her cap and gown, pay her dues for books and get her senior pictures. She could not believe it. She was finished with school. Keysha didn't have any plans but to get out of her mother's house. It was only twelve o'clock in the afternoon. Keysha went home to eat. She didn't have to be back to school for another three hours.

"Mom, are you in here!" she yelled, but there was no answer.

Good. Keysha didn't have to deal with her right now. Keysha was on her way to the refrigerator when the mailman knocked on the door.

"Good afternoon, young lady," he said.

"Good afternoon," she smiled.

He handed her the mail. Keysha flipped through the mail and came upon a letter for her mother. It was from a doctor dealing with mental disorders she found out as she opened the letter.   Keysha looked around and assumed it would be safer for her to read this in a locked room. She ran upstairs. Keysha actually skipped steps to get to her room.

The letter said that Pamela had missed her last eight appointments, and that she needed her medication refills for her disorder. Keysha wondered what disorder she had. This explains it all. This is why she always said things that weren't true and seen things that weren't there.

Maybe that's why she became so abusive to her. Keysha wanted to talk to this doctor; to find out what is the matter with her. Keysha thought against it. Her mother might kill her.

Where did the time go? It's already 2:30, and she had to meet Mr. Johnson at 3:00. So Keysha took the letter and jumped into her black Honda Civic.

She went speeding to school. Keysha didn't want to be late for her meeting. She pulled up to the school, parked, and made a dash for the office.

"Hi, Mrs. Brown. Is Mr. Johnson in?" Keysha said it out of breath. She had ran up the hallway.

"Take a breather, Ms. Williams," she laughed

"I didn't want to be late for my appointment."

"You're okay. He just came into the office anyway."

"Can I go in?"

"Yes."

She walked in and Mr. Johnson was on the phone talking to someone. He motioned for her to sit down. Keysha sat in the chair, slowly crossing her legs, exposing her freshly shaven legs. She caught him staring at them and he quickly turned away. He hung up the phone.

"Keysha. What can I do for you today? Your grades are excellent. So I know that's not the problem," he smiled at her.

"No, Mr. Johnson, it's not me. It's my cousin, Monique."

"Oh. What about Ms. Williams?"

"My cousin is a good person. It's very important that she graduates from school."

"I agree with you that Monique is a good

person. But she is a credit short and has missed numerous days from school."

"Well, you know her situation. Is there anything she can do?"

"I'm afraid not. Her only choice is summer school."

"Well, is there anything that I can do?" she smiled and gave him a seductive look.

"Like what? I don't think so, Ms. Williams, and I think you better leave."

"Are you sure?" she asked.

"Yes, but before you leave, take this piece of paper with you."

He took out a piece of paper and wrote something on it. He folded it up and handed it to her.

"What is this?"

"Open it when you're somewhere private."

Keysha took the piece of paper and put it in her purse. On her way out to the car she remembered to throw away the note she read earlier. Keysha did not want to get a beat down before she graduated this Friday. Once in the

car, she took the note out of her purse and read it.

Meet me at my house at eight o'clock and we can discuss helping your cousin graduate.

"Great, I hope I can pull this off," she said to herself and then her phone rings.

"Who?"

"Damn, baby! Can you just say hello?" Tyrese said.

"Hey, Hun, what's up?" she laughed.

"Oh, that's funny?"

"Yeah, a little."

What are you doing tonight?"

"Nothing." She lied knowing she was going to meet her principal tonight.

"Can we get together?"

"Yeah. Oh, I forgot. I told Monique I would help her with her last minute baby stuff." She couldn't believe she was lying to the man she loved.

"Damn, when are you going to make time for me?" He got angry.

"Stop acting like a baby. I'll try to leave

166

her place early enough to spend time with you. Okay?"

"Okay. You promise?"

"Yes, I promise." She hung up the phone. What the hell was she doing? This is the last time she would sleep with anyone other than Tyrese. She really loved him.

Keysha had to help her cousin out this one last time. She pulled up to her house and just sat in the car. She contemplated actually going through with this. Keysha felt torn between her cousin and her man.

"Keysha! Monique is on the phone!" her mom yelled from the front door.

Keysha ran up the sidewalk and into the house. Her mom handed her the cordless phone and she took it upstairs to her room.

"Hello."

"Hey, girl."

"What's the matter now?"

"I'm not going to graduate and my mom was right. I can't do it all."

"Don't worry about it. Something good will happen. I'm sure of it."

"If I don't graduate Friday, I don't think

I will be able to finish summer school with a new born."

"It will be alright. Trust me."

"But Mr. Lest, the guidance counselor, said..."

"Monique, don't worry about it. I'll call you later. I have a beep, and it's Tyrese."

"Alright later."

* * * * *

"Hello."

"That sounds so much better."

"I thought you might like it. Didn't I just talk to you?"

"Yes. I just wanted to tell you to call me before you came over. I might go visit my father."

"Cool."

"Alright, I'll see you later. I love you."

"I love you, too. See you tonight."

"Umm, I can't wait." Then he hung up.

She went to her closet to get her clothes out for the night. Keysha also packed a bag to stay over Tyrese's tonight. It was already seven and she only had a few minutes to get ready. Keysha had just gotten out of the shower. Her stomach felt funny. She really didn't want to do this. It would be over very soon and then off to her baby's house. She got dressed and grabbed the paper with the address on it as she headed out.

She was in front of the building now. It was now or never. She got out of the car and walked up to the door. She stood there for a few minutes. Then Keysha pushed the doorbell and Mr. Johnson came to the door.

"Hello. Come in."

"Thank you, Mr. Johnson."

"None of that Mr. Johnson stuff. We are equals tonight. It's Andre."

"Okay, Andre," she smiled at him.

"Well, I wasn't sure you would come because you don't even know what I want."

"I wasn't sure I would come either. I'm sure of what you want from me Andre."

"Well, I called and talked to Mr. Lest, the senior guidance counselor. Monique can graduate and walk with her class."

"Thank you, Mr. I mean Andre." She jumped up and hugged him and he started kissing her.

"Let's go upstairs," he said to her.

"Okay."

She was so happy for Monique. Keysha wanted to repay him and she was willing to really sex him good. A proper thank you was in store for this man. They got to the top of the steps and he picked her up and carried her to his room. He was so romantic and gentle just like her man.

Once in the room they kissed and fondled each other. Then she took over. Keysha started sucking on his neck and caressing his dick. She undressed him and licked his back. Keysha could tell he liked this. His eyes were rolling into the back of his head. She took off her clothes. Keysha fell back down on the bed

and spread her legs apart to give him an open invitation into her.

He reached over on the dresser and put on a condom. She liked older men. They didn't need any direction on what to do next. And this nigga had a huge dick.

When Keysha saw the magnum wrapper, her body got a little tense. But she was up for the challenge. He came over and began licking her feet. He licked her legs all the way up to her pussy. She tried not to enjoy it, but he was the most attentive lover she had ever had. He then came up and put his tongue in her ears. Keysha eyes rolled back in her head. Finally he put that big dick inside her. It felt like it was all the way in her stomach. This old motherfucker could stroke. She was climbing the walls. Don't get me wrong, she would handle her's once she conquered the big dick. She got on top of that dick and rode him until he came. She was tired, and so was he. The doorbell rang and she looked at him.

"Who is that?" she whispered.

"Oh, it's probably my son. Don't worry.

You don't know him. What I do is my business. He's not the messy type.

We have a very good relationship."

"I don't know."

"Don't worry about it. Go take a shower. He will be gone by the time you get out."

"Let me go see what he wants."

"Doesn't your son have a key?"

"Yes, but when I have the red light on at the front door, he rings the doorbell."

"Oh, I get it now," she laughed and went to get in the shower. Andre went to go talk to his son.

"What's up, Dad? I see you have company. The red light is on." He gave him some dap.

"Yeah, I have a tender little thing upstairs. I've wanted to hit that pussy for four years now. She's legal now. So you know..." he laughed

"You're going to go to jail fooling with those young girls."

"We are both willing participants. So what brings you out this way?"

"I wanted to hang out with you for a couple of hours while my girl helps her cousin with some baby stuff."

"As long as it's not your baby stuff."

"Dad, hell no."

"Good. You love this girl, don't you?"

"I truly do love her... so much."

"When will I meet her?" he asked.

But before he could get an answer to his question, Keysha walked down to the stairs. She stood there with her mouth open. It was Tyrese. Oh my god! Mr. Johnson was his father.

"Tyrese, I want you to meet..." his dad started to say.

"Keysha Williams." Tyrese looked at her with disgust.

"Yeah. How did you know, Son?"

"This was my girlfriend."

"Tyrese, I didn't know this was your father."

She ran towards him to put her arms

around him. He just pushed her away.

"Son, I didn't know she was your girlfriend. I would never betray you in anyway," he said to Tyrese.

"Dad, I don't blame you. You never met Keysha. If she would had been faithful to me, none of this would have happened. Would it, Keysha?"

"Tyrese, can we please talk about this?"

"Talk about what? You fucking my father?" he screamed in her face.

"I had to do this. I didn't want to, but Monique wouldn't graduate from school."

He looked at her like he wanted to slap the shit out of her. She would have gladly have taken the hit in the face, but she knew he would never hit her, not even now.

"You didn't have to do shit. It's not your responsibility to get Monique out of trouble. She got pregnant."

"Tyrese, please!"

"Fuck you, Keysha. I never want to see your nasty ass again." And he walked out the

door.

She fell to the floor and just cried. Keysha really loved him and now she had lost him forever.

"Keysha, I'm sorry. I didn't know you and Tyrese were together. I would have never told you to come over here." He helped her up.

"No, Andre. I should have known better." She got up and walked out to go anywhere but here.

CHAPTER 9

Today is Keysha's graduation day and she should be happy. All she can think about is Tyrese. He hasn't returned any of her calls this week. She is going to try to call him one last time.

"Hello," he said

"Tyrese, please don't hang up on me," she begged him.

"What do you want?" he said.

"Can we please try and work this out?" Keysha asked him.

"Let me ask you a question."

"Okay."

"Do you love me?"

"Yes. More than anything."

"If you truly loved me, my well-being would have been your number one priority. You think bitches don't try to push up on me? But my heart belonged to you. That came before anything."

"You are first in my life."

"Keysha, please. You need to grow up and find someone willing to play these games with you. Don't call me again." And he hung up.

She sat at her desk and Keysha just cried. She realized that she had messed up. Keysha would never have him in her life ever again.

* * * * *

"What's wrong with you?" her mom asked.

"Nothing, I'm just excited about graduating," she lied to her. She would just put salt in her wound if she told her.

"Well, get yourself together. I can't wait to see your aunt's face when you walk across that stage with honors and Monique walks across with a big belly. She barely got to graduate. I still don't know how they pulled that one off."

"Mom, just be happy for Monique."

"Oh, I am happy for her," she smiled at

me

"Good."

"Well, let's go and get that diploma," she said.

She really didn't want to go. She just wanted to rub it in her aunt's face; that she got Keysha out of high school without getting pregnant.

"Boy, is it crowded at this school today," her mom said.

"We have the biggest graduating class ever."

"I'll see you in the auditorium," she kissed her on the cheek.

That shocked her. She never showed any affection towards Keysha. She walked to the cafeteria to line up with the rest of her class.

As soon as Keysha reached the cafeteria she saw her cousin in line with her huge stomach sticking out. Keysha walked over to her but stopped to give Michelle and Trina a big hug.

"We did it, girl." Trina said.

"Yes, we did," Keysha smiled.

"I am so happy to be getting out of this town," Michelle said to them.

Michelle was going in the Air Force and Trina was headed to Howard University. Trina was very smart. She was the Valedictorian. Keysha gave them one last hug and walked over to get in line.

"I saved you a spot right in front of me," Monique said to her.

"Thanks."

"Are you ready for this?"

"Yes, I am."

"Is Tyrese out there with Aunt Pam?" she asked

"No. Tyrese and I broke up."

"What? Why did y'all break up?"

"I really don't want to get into it right now."

"Okay. Thanks for whatever you said to Principal Johnson."

"No thanks necessary. I love you," she smiled. She really wanted to say, 'Because of you I lost the man I love.'

"Everyone line up. It's time to graduate." Mr. Johnson said. He looked at her and put his head down.

"Keysha Williams." Principal Johnson said. Her mother and Aunt screamed. Principal Johnson never looked at her.

"Monique Williams." Keysha screamed as loud as she could, but not as loud as Davon did.

After the ceremonies everyone poured into the hallways. And Davon ran over to Monique and gave her a big kiss and hug. Keysha was so jealous of her. Her man would have been there if it wasn't for her.

"Congratulations, sweet pea," Jackie said to her.

"Thank you."

"Hello, Jackie," Pam said.

"Hello, Pam. Good job with Keysha," she hugged her.

"Thank you, same too you," she smiled. Keysha was glad that no drama popped off.

"Excuse me, Ms. Jackie," Trina interrupted. "Monique isn't feeling well."

They all ran over to see what was wrong with her. She was bent over holding her stomach. Davon grabbed her and took her to the hospital. Everyone followed behind them. Keysha and Pam sat in the waiting area for hours. Then her aunt and Davon came out.

"The doctors want to keep her overnight," Jackie said.

"Is she alright?" Keysha asked.

"Yeah. They think its false labor, but want to keep her overnight to be sure, because she is so close to her due date," she explained.

"Well, can I see her?" Keysha asked her aunt.

"Yeah. You know she was asking for you."

Keysha walked through the double doors. She looked in the room and saw the monitor on her stomach. It was monitoring the baby's heartbeat.

"You just had to show off at the graduation."

"Shut up and come over here."

"Are you scared?"

"A little."

"It will be over soon. Then it's back to the short skirts and shorts," she told her.

"Girl, I hope I bounce back like that. Can I ask you a favor?"

"Yeah." She thought, 'What now?' Keysha had already fucked the principal for her.

"Will you be my baby's god mother? I want you to name her."

"Yeah," Keysha was a little choked up.

"It's a girl. Don't tell anybody. Davon and I wanted to keep it a secret. But you know I can't hide anything from you," she hugged her.

"Well, I can name her anything?"

"Anything that sounds good," she looked at Keysha.

"Okay. What about Harmony?"

"Keysha, I like that. I'm going to name her Harmony."

"What if it's a boy?'

"We will name him Harmony," they both laughed

"I'm going to leave, so you can get some rest."

"Are you going to the party tonight?"

"I don't think so. I'm tired."

"Girl, you should be shaking your tail feather. You don't have any kids," she laughed.

"I might go out. I don't know."

"Please, do something. I don't want you to just sit home doing nothing," she said.

Before dozing off from the medicine, Keysha covered her up and walked back out to the waiting room.

"Mom, you ready?" she asked her.

"Yeah, let's go," she said. It looked like something had happened while she was with Monique.

"Is Monique still up?" Davon asked.

"No. She fell asleep talking to me," she told him.

"Good night, Auntie," Keysha kissed her on the cheek.

"Good night, Keysha." She looked at Pam and walked away.

"What was that all about?" she asked Pam.

"I don't know. But let's go."

They got back to the house and Keysha was happy. She had had a long draining week. Her mom decided to go over Colin's tonight. So that left Keysha by herself for the night, as usual. She turned her cell phone back on, just in case her aunt tried to reach her in the middle of the night. Keysha took off all her clothes and fell asleep.

Keysha's cell phone is ringing. She looked over at the clock. It was one o'clock in the morning. She thought it must have been her aunt calling about Monique."

"Hello."

"What's up, Keysha?" the voice said.

"What's up? Are you okay?"

"Yeah. Can I see you tonight?"

"For what."

"Can I be honest with you?"

"Yeah. I like honesty."

"I've been wanting to fuck you since the first day I met you four years ago. But I figured you were out of my league."

"But you have a girlfriend."

"I know. I love my girlfriend. But I want to fulfill my last fantasy of being with you before I take the plunge. Will you spend one night with me?"

"I don't know about this."

"Nobody will ever have to know about this."

"I'll be right over."

"Good. Get ready for a freaky night," and he hung up.

Keysha hung up the phone, showered and headed out for her night of fun, making sure to grab her cell phone just in case. She pulled up to the apartment and turned off the car. She wanted this guy just as much as he wanted her. Keysha knocked on the door. He opened the door completely naked. He grabbed her by the shirt and jerked her in. She immediately dropped to her knees and started sucking his dick. This is something she never did with anyone but Tyrese. He was moaning. He then turned around and spread his ass cheeks apart. She began to lick his ass. He loved it.

The fact that he was so into it turned her so on that Keysha couldn't even begin to explain. He then undressed her and began eating her pussy. Next, he asked Keysha if he could slap her. That's what he was into. She said yes and this nigga slapped the fuck out of her. That really turned him on. He snatched her off the floor and put one of her legs on the table. And he started fucking her from behind as hard as he could.

"Take this dick, you bitch," he said to her.

"Fuck me, you bastard," she said to him. This seemed to turn him even more.

He was pulling her hair, slapping her ass and biting her. He sat in a chair and told her to ride him until he came. Keysha went to get a condom out of her purse, but he stopped her and pulled Keysha on top of him. She rode him and sucked his neck. He instructed Keysha not to put any hickies on his neck. He finally came. She had come several times already. She got up and put her clothes on, sticky and all.

Keysha headed for the door as her

phone rang.

"Hello," she said.

"Hey, Keysha. It's Auntie."

"Is everything okay?" Keysha asked her

"Yeah. Monique is about to have the baby. She wants you here."

"Okay. I'm on my way."

"Could you do me a favor and call Davon. He went home to take a shower, and he's not answering his phone."

"Yes, Auntie I can do that. I'll be there in few minutes."

As Keysha was walking out of the door she turned around.

"Davon. Monique's is getting ready to have the baby," she told him.

"Okay. I'll meet you at the hospital."

"Alright," Keysha shut his door and headed for the hospital.

CHAPTER 10

Well it's been exactly nine months since Keysha told her mother she was pregnant. And she put her out the same week. Keysha had already made her arrangements to have her place before she told her. So she simply gathered her things and moved into her apartment. It was two buildings behind Monique and Davon's place. She was lucky that she didn't have to spend any of her money to pay for the furnishings of the place. Thanks to James and his generosity she was set. Keysha had only days until her baby will be born. She needed to head out to pick up some last minute things.

Keysha could not believe how much baby things cost. She had said this out loud. The lady standing next to her was pregnant and must have been thinking the same thing.

"Girl, I know that's right," she said

"Aren't these prices ridiculous?" Keysha

laughed.

"How many months are you?" she asked.

"Nine. But I feel like twelve month's pregnant. How far along are you?"

"I'm only seven months along, but I feel you."

"Do you know what you're having?" Keysha asked her.

"A boy. What about you?"

"A girl. So do you have a name picked out yet."

"Yes. This one is going to be a junior," she said to Keysha. She started to tell her the name when Tyrese walked up. She thought to herself, 'Damn, I don't feel like explaining anything to him.'

"Hey, baby, you found everything you need for the baby?" he asked.

"Yes, Tyrese," the lady answered.

"Good. Only the best for our son," he kissed her on the cheek.

"Oh, this is my baby daddy," she said and started laughing.

"Hi," Keysha said, like she didn't know

him.

"Hi," he said to Keysha. He turned to the mother of his child. "Baby, let's go."

"Okay, boo," she kissed him.

"Nice to have met you." she said.

After that encounter, all she wanted to do was go home and forget about the day. Keysha put everything back. She would get it later. She drove back to the apartment. Keysha waddled up the stairs to her place and went in.

She looked around and thought, 'This is the last time this place will ever be quiet again.' Keysha reached in her pocket because her cell phone was vibrating. She looked at the name and it was Tyrese.

"Hello."

"Hi, Keysha," he said

"What do you want?'

"I want to know if the baby you're carrying is mine," he demanded.

"Why would you think that?" she asked him.

"You're right. Why would I.? Well, let

me put it another way. Is that my son or daughter you're carrying?" He said to her.

"You can be a real bastard. No, this baby belongs to my fiancée. We are very happy. So please don't ever call me again," she said.

"Believe me, I won't," and he hung up.

As soon as Keysha got off the phone with him, her stomach began to hurt. Next thing, her panties felt wet. Her water had broken, and she was in labor. She opened her cell phone. She called Monique to ask to take her to the hospital. Monique was so excited. She was the baby's godmother.

Once at the hospital Keysha acted like a damn fool. She was in labor for twenty-three hours. Damn near a whole day.

"Keysha, she is beautiful," Monique said holding her.

"She is. Isn't she, Monique?" she asked.

"She has green eyes, just like Harmony."

"Yeah, she does, Keysha said, thinking, 'Just like her daddy.'

"So, don't you want to know?" Monique smiled at her.

"Know what?" she asked.

"The name I picked out for her," she smiled.

"Yes. What is my daughter's name anyway?"

"Treasure. Do you like it?" she asked her.

"Monique, that is beautiful. I bet you really took your time to figure out a name for her."

"Of course, I did. This is our family we are talking about," she was so excited about being the godmother.

"Yeah, that's true," Keysha said to her, feeling a little drowsy.

"Look I'll take her back to the nursery, and I'll pick the both of you up tomorrow," she came over and gave her a kiss on the forehead.

"Yeah, I am tired. Thank you for being here with me."

"Where else would I be? But I better get home. I've been here for over thirty hours. Davon is going to cuss me out."

"That bitch better not," she sat up.

"Keysha, I'm playing," she looked at her.

"Oh, okay. You better be playing," she smiled. She took Treasure and Keysha fell asleep.

While driving home from the hospital Monique decide to pick up a pizza, because she was too tired to cook tonight. She pulled up to the apartment complex. Monique was so happy to be home because she needed to take a shower.

"Hey, babe. I'm back. I got some pizza for dinner tonight," she said to Davon.

"Damn. I thought you were going to move into the hospital," he said to her.

"Keysha finally had the baby about two hours ago," she told him. Monique walked over to the table to put the pizza on it.

"Really? That's good," he said, not really sounding interested.

"She had a girl, and I named her treasure."

"Really? Are you going to ask were your own daughter is?"

"Yeah. Where is Harmony?" she asked

him.

"My sister is keeping her tonight, so we can have some time alone, if you know what I mean..." he smiled at her while squeezing her breast.

"Yes, I know what you mean," she leaned in and kissed him.

"That's what I'm talking about."

"Tomorrow I'll take Harmony to see the baby," she said.

"You're really into this baby. What? You want another one?" he looked at her.

"No I don't want another baby. I only have six more months of school left. Anyway, I think Harmony is enough right now."

"The way you keep going on about Keysha's baby. I can't tell," he raised his eyebrow.

"No, it's not that. Keysha's daughter looks so much like Harmony it's uncanny. She has green eyes. If I didn't know any better, you could be her father," she said, starting to laugh.

"That shit's not funny. I don't even like your fucking cousin. She is a trifling-ass whore. Who doesn't know who her baby's father is?" he said, going off.

Monique looked at him like he was crazy. What the hell was wrong with him?

"Are you alright?" she asked him

"Yeah. I just need some fresh air. I've been in this house all day," He kissed her and left.

* * * * *

Keysha was sleeping in the hospital room when someone tapped her on the shoulders. She looked up and saw that it was Davon.

"What do you want?" Keysha asked with an attitude.

"I came to see the baby," he looked at her

"For what? You don't fuck with me like

that."

"She really is mine, isn't she?" he asked her.

"Yes, but I tried to tell you that," she told him.

"I don't want Monique to find out," he said to her.

"Me neither. She is very good to me and I don't want to hurt her," she said.

"Good, then we are in agreement. I'll give you money for her. But I don't want anything to do with you," he told her. Then he walked out the door.

The next morning Monique was there bright and early. She was ready before the doctor had come to release them. She drove Keysha and the baby home and helped her get settled.

Monique held Treasure the entire time. Then there was a knock on the door. Monique handed Keysha the baby and went to answer the door.

"Who is it?" Monique called out.

"It's Aunt Pam, Monique." Keysha's

mother said.

She looked back at Keysha. She motioned for Monique to open the door. Pam came in with a pink stuffed pig and a balloon. Keysha couldn't believe it. She hasn't fooled with her the whole time she was pregnant. She came over and gave Keysha a kiss and asked to hold the baby.

"Isn't she beautiful?" Monique said to her.

"She is," Pam said

"Mom, what are you doing out this way?" Keysha asked her.

"Can't I come see my granddaughter?" she said to her.

"Of course you can," she didn't want to start any shit today.

"What's her name?"

"Treasure. Monique named her," Keysha said. Just then Treasure opened her eyes.

"Her eyes are green. Girl, she is going to make you some money when she gets older," she said, so nonchalantly.

"What the fuck did you say? Give me my baby,"

she said, taking the baby from her and giving her to Monique.

"What's wrong with your motherfucking-ass?" she yelled.

"I'm not going to turn my daughter into a fucking whore like you tried to do me," she yelled at her.

"Everybody has to make their money," she said to her.

"Get out before I kill you," Keysha told her.

"Your ass ain't gonna do shit."

"Stay right there. You ain't said nothing but a word." Keysha said to her while walking to her room.

"Keysha, what are you doing?" Monique screamed.

She came back out with her piece. Monique ran past her with the baby and shut the door.

"Now you listen to me, bitch," she said to Pam. "You can walk out of here or get carried out in a body bag. This is my house. I run shit here. You better remember it."

"You are crazy. I didn't mean anything by it," she said backing up to the door.

"If I'm crazy, you made me that way. Now get the fuck out."

She grabbed the doorknob and ran out.

Keysha walked over and locked the door.

Monique came out of the room.

"You are one crazy bitch."

CHAPTER 11

Keysha was truly feeling the sting of having a baby. It had been six months and she was back at work. She had so many bills! Keysha didn't realize the enormous responsibility of taking care of a baby. Keysha wouldn't get paid until next Friday and there was only one can of formula in the cupboard. That wouldn't last her through the night. She had to do something; her baby needed food. She needed to make some calls. Her first call was to Monique. No one answered at home and she didn't answer her cell phone. Davon hadn't come over with the money yet that he gave her every week. She couldn't reach him either. Next she tried James. Again there was no answer. She couldn't believe it. She would have to call her mother. This is was her last resort. She bundled Treasure up and headed out to her mother's.

She pulled up to the building and started to have second thoughts. Then she looked over to her daughter and realized that she had no choice. Keysha got out of the car and went around to the backseat of her car to take her daughter out. She walked up to the door and knocked.

"Who is it?" her mom yelled.

"It's me, Mom," Keysha answered.

Pam opened the door, looking a little shocked that it was her daughter. She just stood there, not even inviting them in. Her hands were on her hips and she looked at her. Keysha could tell she was still mad that she had pulled a gun on her.

"What are you doing here?" she said to her.

"I can't come and see you now?" she asked her.

"I guess. After the last incident I thought we were through with each other," her mom reminded her.

"Can we come in?" she asked her.

"Yeah, come on in," she said and moved over to allow them to pass.

Keysha walked in the house. Nothing had changed. The house still looked the same. Pam walked past her and sat down in a chair.

"Okay, Keysha, what do you want?" she said to her.

"Why do you think I want something?" she asked her.

"After our last encounter...," she started.

"I just wanted to bring the baby by, so you could see her," she said.

"Keysha, I know where you stay at. If I wanted to see my granddaughter I would have come over or called. But you made it very clear. You didn't want to have anything to do with me," she just looked at her.

"Well, Treasure needs some milk until Friday. Can you help me out? I'll pay you back on Friday when I get paid," Keysha said to her.

"Oh, well, the truth comes out, and I knew you were not just in the neighborhood. Well, let me tell you like this. You told me to leave you and your baby alone. I'm going to do

just that. So the answer is no," She said to Keysha without cracking so much as a smile.

"Do you even care about your grandchild?" she yelled at her.

"Did I tell you to have that baby? No, I didn't. I told you not to have any kids; that it would ruin your life. Didn't I?" she yelled at her.

"You know what? I don't know why I fucking even came over here!" Keysha wanted to cry.

"I don't, either," Pam looked at her.

"I can't believe you," Keysha said to her. She bundled up Treasure and started walking to the door.

"I know how you can make a quick three hundred dollars if you want it," her mother said to her. Keysha just stood there. She really wanted to stop sleeping around for money, but what choice did she have right now?

"Who is it, Mom?" she asked her.

"Mr. Jones," she said.

"Can you watch her until I come back?" Keysha asked her.

"No, I cannot. You will have to take her with you, just like I had to do with you," she told her. Keysha just looked at her.

Keysha walked out the door and started to get in the car. She looked down at her daughter sleeping and looked at the Jones's house. She walked over to the house and rang the doorbell.

"Hi, Mr. Jones. My mother tells me you are looking for me," she said.

"Yes, I was. Is this a good time?" he said looking down at her daughter.

"This is the only time I have," she told him.

"Well, come in and lay her on the couch," he said.

Mr. Jones got right down to it. Keysha hadn't had sex since she gave birth. Her pussy was tight. He took her clothes off and started to eat her pussy. Keysha must admit she was

just as horny as he was. She sat him in the chair and started to ride him. Then he asked her to fuck him up the ass. Keysha started to wonder if Mr. Jones was on the down low.

"How would I do that?" she asked him. He got up and went to his room. He returned with a vibrator.

"With this," he said.

The man came back with a nine-inch long dildo. He had it all lubricated and ready to go. She took it. He bent over the chair and spreads his ass cheeks apart. Keysha stuck the dildo in his ass just like he instructed her to do.

"Do you like it, baby?" she asked him. Keysha stood there, bored as hell, just pushing the dildo in and out.

"Oh, yeah, baby. Deeper, deeper!" he begged her.

"Like this?" she asked him.

"Yes!" he screamed like a little bitch. Mr. Jones' ass was like a whole in a doughnut. This man was a professional. Keysha hand-fucked him until he came.

"Thank you," he said to her.

"No problem," she told him. And then Keysha got dressed to leave. Instead of giving her three hundred dollars, he gave her five.

"I know it's hard for you right now, and I know your crazy-ass mother isn't helping you," he said to her.

"Thank you," she kissed him on the cheek.

"Just call when you want to make a couple of dollars," he told her on the way out of the door.

Keysha got into the car and realized she might have to go back to her old ways, for a little while anyway.

She pulled up in front of the grocery store and took her baby in. She got the formula and a couple of other things she needed and headed straight for home.

Once Keysha got in the house, which was a struggle with carrying the baby seat and groceries, but she did it. There were four calls on her machine, all from Monique.

"Hey, cuz, are you all right? I just got

your message. Call me," she said, sounding concern.

"Keysha, where are you? Did something happen to Treasure? Girl, call me when you get in," she said.

Before Keysha could listen to the other two messages, she called again.

"Hello?" Keysha said

"Hey, are you okay? You sounded funny on the message you left me," Monique asked her.

"I'm fine now. Let me call you right back. I just got in. I need to wash your god-daughter and put up some groceries," she told her.

"Okay. Call me back, or I'll be over there," she said to Keysha and she meant it to.

* * * * *

The house was finally at ease. Keysha was in her nightclothes and very comfortable in bed when there was a knock at the door. She thought to herself, 'It's Monique.' She had

forgot to call her.

"Who is it?" she asked.

"As if you didn't know," Monique said to her.

Keysha opened up the door. Monique was tapping her foot and had her hands on her hips.

"Thanks for calling me back," she walked past her.

"Come on in," Keysha said, shutting the door.

"I could tell something was wrong with you on the phone," Monique said.

"Come on in the room with me and we can talk," she told her.

She followed Keysha to the room. They lay down in the bed like they used to during their teenage years.

"So, what's up?" She said.

"Well I just was feeling low, but I'm fine now," she told her.

"Feeling low about what?" she inquired.

"I didn't have any money to get Treasure her formula. My mom and I got into it because

she wouldn't help me. You know, the usual," Keysha told her.

"Why didn't you call me?" she asked.

"I did. Remember?" she said

"I mean... You know what I mean," she laughed.

"I know but I got some money. I'm alright," Keysha told her.

"Where did you get the money from?" she asked.

"You don't want to know."

"Yeah, your right. I brought you some money anyway." She pulled out two hundred dollars.

"I can't take your money. Anyway, I have my own money now."

"Well, it's not my money exactly," she told her.

"Whose is it?" Keysha asked.

"Davon gave it to me. And don't try and interrupt me. He said he wanted you to have it regardless, even if the two of you don't like each other; that it has everything to do with Treasure," Monique looked at her.

"Okay. Tell him thank you." Keysha told her. She was thinking that the nigga was supposed to have given her this money two days ago.

"Well, I have to go. I have a lot of studying to do," she said.

"I can't believe you just graduated and you're already back in school again," she told her.

"I know. I really want to make money and going for a four year degree will help me. You should think about going to school, too. You are so smart and it will benefit you and Treasure in the end. Plus, you can go for just two years," she smiled at her.

"I'll think about it," she hugged her and said good night.

CHAPTER 12

Thank goodness it was Friday and the
week was over.   Let the weekend
begin.   Keysha had just been promoted to
supervisor at work, thanks to the extra hours
she put in with the manager. She had been
giving away sexual favors to make it to the top.
She looked at the clock and noticed it was time
to get up for work. Treasure stayed over at
Monique's house last night. She didn't have to
rush into work today. Keysha realized that her
bed was wet again. She had been waking up
with night sweats for last six months. Keysha
got up to change her sheets and take a shower.
After getting herself ready for work, she
noticed the rent check still on the dresser.

        "Hi, Travis," she said to the manager of
her complex.

        "Hey, Keysha, going off to work
already?" he said to her.

        "I just came by to drop off my check for

rent," she smiled.

He got up and locked the office door. Travis put the closed sign in the window. He turned around and started to kiss her.

"Turn on your answering machine. You'll be a little busy for a minute," Keysha smiled at him.

He turned on the answering machine and followed her into the other room. Once in the room, Keysha took over. She grabbed Travis by his tie and started licking his neck. He pulled her skirt up and reached for her panties but Keysha wasn't wearing any. She had planned on fucking him anyway.

"Damn, were you ready for me.?" he asked her.

"You know I was," she stuck her tongue in his mouth.

Travis picked Keysha up and put her on the desk. He pulled down his pants. She reached in her pocket and gave him a condom.

"You don't play around, do you?" he asked.

"You damn right. I only have one life," she told him.

He put the condom on and raised her legs up over his shoulders and went deep from the jump. He was just pumping away. Keysha acted like he was killing her. He then told her to get on all fours. He was doing her from behind. Keysha was wondering if her mom would change her mind and not watch Treasure tonight. Today was Monique's bachelorette party. The last time her mom watched her was six months ago.

"Oh, yes, Travis. This shit feels good," she lied.

"Yeah, take that shit, baby," he said.

Keysha had been fucking Travis for a year now, ever since the complex hired a new property manager. Keysha has not paid rent in a year. Travis was finished. She had to shower again and head off to work. Keysha turned around and kissed him, to make it seem like the sex was off the chain. This mug fell for it every time.

"Same time, same place next week?" he said to her as he handed her check back to Keysha.

"You know it," she kissed him and tore up the check.

"Aw shit, I'm late for work."

Keysha hurried up out of the shower and threw on her new suit. She bought last week. Keysha jumped in her car and took off, speeding the whole way to work. She parked and walked hastily into the building. She went to her office to print out the reports when the manager who promoted her came in.

"Hey, I just came to say goodbye," he smiled.

"Nathan, I am going to miss you," she smiled at him.

"I'm going to miss you too. We still on for lunch?" he asked

"Yes. I was running a little late, but I always have time for you." Keysha said to him, "Ladies don't ever burn their bridges."

He left and she got back to work. Keysha was so into her work that she didn't realize how much time had passed. It was already lunchtime, but she was leaving early anyway. The party tonight was at her place and her girls, Michelle and Trina, were coming early to help her set up. Keysha shut her computer down and went to find Nathan for their lunch date.

Keysha followed Nathan out of the parking lot to go eat lunch. She noticed that he passed all the restaurants. They pulled up in front of his condo. He stepped out of his jeep and came over to her car. Keysha rolled her window down and gave him a seductive look.

"What's up with this? Lunch at your house?" she asked him.

"Yeah, this is the last weekend before I leave for New York. You said I could have anything for lunch; it was on you. And I plan to eat you well today," he licked his lips.

"Damn, how can I pass up that offer?" she smiled and got out of the car.

She walked into his house.   There were boxes everywhere. Nathan shut the door behind her. He grabbed her hand and led her to the balcony.

"Why are we out here?" she asked him.

"Just sit down. I'll be right back," he told her.

He came back with strawberries, whipped cream, champagne and wine glasses. Nathan dipped the strawberries in the whipped cream and fed one to her. He poured her a glass of champagne.

"Stand up," Nathan ordered.

She stood up and he pulled off her skirt. The he took off her panties but told her to leave on her heels. He pushed Keysha back into the chair. Nathan took each of her legs and put them on the arms of the chair. Now she was spread eagle. He gave Keysha a glass of champagne.

"Finish up.   I'm about to eat my dessert," he said.

Nathan put whipped cream on her pussy, took a strawberry, stuck it in her pussy and ate it. Keysha sat there and watched him, sipping her champagne.

"Hand me another strawberry," he told her.

He took the strawberry and rubbed it in her pussy and handed it to her. Keysha reached for it. She took her fingers and rubbed her clit. She had cream and juice all over it. Keysha stuck her fingers in his mouth and he sucked them clean. This started to turn her on. He pulled her up and bent her over the patio table. Nathan told her to spread her ass open wide and then he poured champagne over it. Then he licked it up. She really began to moan and come. They hadn't even fucked yet. Keysha raised her head. She noticed across the field that Nathan's neighbors were watching them. It was a white couple and the man was getting off on what he saw. He was jerking himself off. His girlfriend was fingering herself. They were already naked. Keysha guessed they were tanning.

The next thing she knew, he was banging the fuck out of her. At this very moment Nathan put on a condom and started banging the fuck out of her. Now he has a big dick unlike Travis's. There's no faking it with Nathan. Keysha looked over at the couple. They seem to be enjoying themselves.

They weren't looking at them anymore. He was fucking the shit out of her. Nathan stopped and they moved into the house, to his bedroom. The bed was still up and he laid her on it. He lit a candle and poured the hot wax on her. It stung a little bit, but it didn't kill her. Next he tied Keysha's hands to the bedpost and her feet to the bottom post. He liked some kinky sex, and so did she. Nathan climbed on top of her, spread her legs even further and started to fuck her again. He was extremely horny.

"Keysha, I want to try something with you I've never tried before," he stated.

"Like what?" She was scared because he was a real freak.

"Let me fuck you in the ass," he begged.

Keysha was horny, but, damn, not that horny. And he had a huge dick.

"Nathan, I don't know about that. I've never done that before and I heard it hurts," she told him

"Come on. This is the last time I'll see you. I'll be gentle."

She just sat there and finally agreed that they could try it. She told him that if it was too painful he would have to stop. He untied her and went and got some KY jelly. He greased his dick heavy and then he opened her legs and lathered her as well. Keysha got on all fours. He told her that she wasn't ready to take it that way yet. So Keysha laid on her back. He was trying and trying. It started to hurt a little. Keysha was thinking, 'How does a gay man do this shit all the time?' He finally got in and started to go to work. Keysha was in pain at first, but then she started to like it. Nathan loved it. That nigga was fucking her ass like it was a pussy. She was so happy when he was finished. Her ass was sore.

Keysha started to wonder would she

shit on herself. She got up, took a shower and set out to get ready for the party tonight.

Keysha got home.   Her ass was still throbbing. She ran me some hot water in the tub. Keysha just sat there soaking and hoping the throbbing would stop. The phone rang and she reached for it.

"Speak to me," Keysha said.

"Hey, hooker, what's up?" Michelle said.

"Where are you?" Keysha asked her.

"Trina and me are at the door," she said.

"Okay, let me get out of the tub and come open the door," she said. Keysha got up and put on her robe. She went to the door and opened it.

"Hey, bitches! What's new?" she said to Michelle and Trina.

"Nothing. Damn, can a sister come in?" Trina yelled.

"Come on," she told her. Keysha shut the door behind them.

Trina had already made herself at home. She had taken off her shoes and was lying on the sofa. She looked really good, too.

Her hair was long and gorgeous. Her skin was flawless and she had on the nicest shit. Michelle had gained so much weight. Damn, one thigh was Keysha's whole damn body. She still looked good, though.

"So what do we need to do?" Michelle asked.

"Everything." Keysha said.

"Everything? Like what?" Trina sat up.

"Damn your lazy ass! We have to get the food together. The strippers will be here at six to set up."

"Yeah, that's what I'm talking about!" Trina screamed.

"We thought your nasty-ass would love that," Michelle said.

"How many strippers are you talking about?" Trina asked.

"Shit, Trina, get off the strippers, please. We need to move this furniture out of the way. The DJ will be here at six, also. Michelle, can you start cooking the food? I have already made all the cold salads. Trina, if you can get your mind off of dick long enough, can you

rearrange the furniture?" Keysha ordered.

Everybody put their hand in. "One, two, three," she said.

"Hooker night!" they all yelled.

Keysha went to get dressed. No pussy action tonight for her. The way her ass felt right then, tonight Keysha was strictly a hostess. She came out her room dressed. Something smelled good. Michelle was in the kitchen tearing it up. Trina had the stereo blasting and was in the living room dancing up a storm. She had the living room beautiful. There were balloons, streamers and 'Congratulations' signs everywhere.

"Hey Trina, Michelle, come here," Keysha yelled.

"Yeah," Michelle said.

"Look, Trina can't even hear because she has that damn music on so loud," she said.

Keysha walked over to turn down the stereo. Trina grabbed her and started dancing. Michelle came over and started to get her dance on, too. They danced until they were all out of breath.

"Alright, let's go get dressed before the DJ and strippers get here," Keysha said all out of breath.

They turned around and danced their asses to the back of the house to get dressed. Everybody was there and the DJ had the party right. Monique was all smiles but wouldn't be after the strippers came out. She really didn't want any. Well, Davon didn't want her to have any. Keysha already knew that he was having some at his party. Keysha saw it as fair game.

"Hey, girl, are you enjoying your party?" she asked Monique.

"Yes, thank you. I love you so much," she was slobbering.

"Damn, how many drinks has she had?" Keysha asked.

"It's a party, ain't it?" Trina said.

The DJ started playing some club music. That's the Maryland club shit; music from his home. There was the cue for the strippers to come out of the room. Monique's eyes got big as shit. They came out with hard

dicks in a room full of horny ass bitches.

Keysha looked at Trina who was getting her breast sucked by Chocolate Thunder. This man was black as midnight and beautiful. There were woman grabbing and feeling everything. Michelle was sitting on the bar chair getting her feet sucked. A brother came towards Keysha. She turned him away. Keysha went to the back to get the stripper she had especially for Monique. His name was Kingdom Cum. Keysha just wanted to come looking at him. He was 6'4, with a rock-hard body, and a 10-inch dick. Damn, does she need to say anymore?

"Okay, freaks," she yelled. "I have someone special for Monique tonight."

"Keysha, I told you I didn't want strippers," she whispered to her.

"I think you'll like this," she told her. Kingdom Cum came out of the room. He was pumping his hips up and down. He went over to Monique and started licking her neck. She looked a little scared.

Monique saw that 10 inches. He picked

her up and was pushing his dick up against her pussy. Then he threw her on his shoulders and carried her away to my room. The girls started to scream and the party continued. It was like a big orgy in her house. Everyone was dancing and having a good time, and Keysha forgot that her cousin wasn't back at the party. So she went to check on her scared ass. Keysha went to her room and knocked on the door. There was no answer. She opened the door and would not have believed it if she hadn't seen it with her own eyes. Keysha saw Monique up against the wall and Kingdom Cum was fucking the shit out of her. And to her surprise she was taking it. She just shut the door and turned around. Michelle was standing there.

"Damn, I guess the liquor really took over," Michelle said.

"Yeah, I guess. This is between me and you alright," she said.

"You know I love Monique and you both. And shit, we girls. What happens here stays here." she said.

"That's my girl. Hey, let's not tell Trina."

Keysha said.

"Yes, let's not. We don't want Monique to not get married. You know she still wants Davon. This would be her prime opportunity to go and run and tell," Michelle said.

They returned to the party, or rather, the orgy. It seemed like everybody was fucking. Keysha couldn't find Trina, so she went through the house looking for her. Keysha found her all right. She was in her daughter's room fucking Chocolate Thunder and eating Kelly's ass.

Keysha could not believe it. Trina was bisexual! No wonder her and Kelly seemed so tight in school. Trina glanced up at her and looked embarrassed.

"Hey. Y'all all grown up in here. Handle your business," Keysha said to her.

She smiled at her and continued to eat the hell out of Kelly's ass while Chocolate Thunder never stopped fucking her from behind. Keysha went to the kitchen to eat.

"Hey, big head," Monique said to her.

"I don't think I'm the one with a big

head. That would be Kingdom Cum," Keysha laughed.

"Shut up! Don't laugh. I'm a slut, right?" she asked.

"How you figure that?" she asked.

"I fucked another man days before I am supposed to marry Davon," she said.

"Was the dick good?" she asked.

"Girl, hell yeah!" she smiled.

"Well, shit, I didn't see anything and as far as I'm concerned, you didn't do shit but sat around talking about Davon all night," Keysha hugged her.

They both sat down and ate. Then Keysha told her about Trina and Kelly.

"No wonder that bitch always had an attitude with me. She wanted to eat my pussy," she laughed.

"Oh, yeah. Michelle saw you fucking, too." Keysha told her.

"Damn," she put her head in her hands.

"She said, 'What happens here, stays here,'" she said.

"Good."

They went back in the living room. It smelled like pussy and cologne. People were passed out everywhere as the strippers were packing up, ready to leave. The DJ was in the bathroom with Michelle. When he came back he told Keysha that she didn't have to pay; her girl took care of him. She thought about putting all these freaks out but decided to let everyone stay. Keysha told Michelle they could all sleep in her room.

"Let me change my sheets first," she looked over at Monique.

"Fuck you," she said.

"Yeah, he was fucking the shit out of you," Keysha said.

"He was killing your ass in there," Michelle said.

"What do you expect? He had a ten inch dick?" she yelled.

Keysha changed her sheets and Michelle, Monique and her climbed into the king size bed. They started to have girl talk like when were little. It felt just like one of their sleepovers.

"I can't believe something," Michelle said.

"What?" Monique and Keysha said.

"Keysha didn't fuck anyone tonight," she said.

"Fuck you. I do want to thank you Michelle for paying the DJ in pussy money. Treasure could use that money," she said.

"Girl, anything to help a best friend," she said.

"Well I did have some action earlier. That's why I was avoiding the dick like the plague," Keysha said.

"What did you do?" Monique said.

"Wait, let me put my shorts on," she said

"You still have those purple spots on you?" Monique asked.

"Yeah. I have an appointment on Monday," she told her. "Okay, let me tell y'all what happened." All eyes were on her. "Alright, you and Monique know how I fucked Nathan and he promoted me, right?" she said.

"Yeah!" they both said.

"Well, today was his last day at work,

and he wanted to have lunch with me. I thought we were going to some restaurant. Instead, we went back to his house. We got in the house and he took me out on the balcony. He left me there and brought back strawberries, whip cream and champagne. Girl, he put the whip cream on my pussy. Then he dipped the strawberry inside my pussy and ate it.

"Damn, Keysha, you always have the good sex," Michelle interrupted.

"Wait girl. That's not the half of it. Then he poured champagne in my pussy and sucked it out," Keysha started laughing.

"That's so nasty," Monique said.

"This from a girl who just fucked a man with a ten inch dick days before her wedding. You should not judge. Keysha continue," Michelle said and Monique shut up.

"Okay, anyway, I looked across the field and a white couple was looking at us. They start fucking, too. Anyway, that's not why I didn't get mine today, because you know I can fuck many a nigga in one day. I'm sore because I let

Nathan fuck me in the ass. It was the first time I did it," she told them.

"Girl, what? I always have anal sex with Jeff. Did you like it?" Michelle asked her.

"After I got past the pain, I kind of enjoyed it."

"No wonder you were avoiding dick today," Monique said.

"You really shouldn't talk," Keysha told Monique.

"Whatever. I'm going to sleep because the two of you are going to ride me all night."

"You mean all day! It's six o'clock in the morning," Michelle said, "I'm going to sleep too.

"Me too," Keysha said.

"Thank you both for a great night," Monique said, and then fell asleep.

CHAPTER 13

Keysha was so excited. She was meeting Monique for breakfast today to tell her that she wanted to register for college. Keysha could not believe she was about to do something with her life.

"Hey, girl. What is the emergency that I had to call my job and say that I'm going to be late?" Monique said to her.

"I have a surprise to tell you," Keysha told her.

"Don't tell me Kingdom Cum is looking for me," she laughed.

"No, but I think you're stuck on that big dick of his!" she laughed at her.

"Maybe, but can you blame me?" Monique smiled at her.

"Anyway, enough about dicks. I wanted to meet with you today because I want you to go with me to register for college today," Keysha told her. She jumped out of her seat and gave her a big hug.

"So, I finally wore you down, huh?" she

smiled at Keysha.

"Yeah, I guess," she admitted.

"So, have you decided what you're going to take?" she asked.

"Yes. Psychology. I want to help people like me." She said. "Why are you staring at me like that? Please don't cry, Monique."

"I am so proud of you. I knew I had seen a change in you." She grabbed her hands.

"Thanks for showing me there is life outside the bedroom. And let go of my hands before people think we are like Trina!" Keysha laughed

"You are crazy. Hey do you have purple spots on your hand now?" she asked her.

"Yeah. I don't know what's going on. I have a doctor's appointment today. Okay, enough about being sick. Let's go register for my classes."

"Okay, you don't have to tell me twice."

"Hey, Monique? I also need a ride to the college. My car is in the shop and won't be ready til after twelve," Keysha asked.

"Girl to register for school? How could I

say no?"

They jumped into her Escalade and sped off to the college. Once Keysha got there she became so nervous. She went to get her paperwork and filled it out. Keysha walked up to the cashier and wrote out a check for her classes. She turned around and headed toward Monique who had her arms stretched out.

"How does it feel?" Monique asked.

"I feel like I finally accomplished something." Keysha began to cough.

"What time is your appointment?" she asked.

Keysha looked down at her watch. "In about forty five minutes. Could you give me a ride?" she asked Monique.

Monique pulled up to the office building to drop Keysha off.

"Do you want me to wait for you? I'm already late anyway." She seemed so concerned about Keysha.

"No, no. I can catch the bus home," she told Monique

"Call me as soon as you get home," she

told her.

Keysha walked up the stairs and into the doctor's office. Keysha signed in and sat down. Keysha was really tired today.

"Ms. Williams," the nurse called for her. "Dr. Delgatto will see you now."

"Thank you," Keysha replied. She led her to a room to wait.

"She will be right with you," she told her.

Keysha hated the doctor's office because you always had to hurry up and wait. She wondered what was wrong. With this cold and these spots, she hoped it was just the flu. The room was so cold; the white walls and bed with the paper sheets. She just didn't like this feeling. There was a knock on the door.

"Hi, Ms. Williams. How are you?" Dr. Delgatto asked.

"Great, Dr. D. I'll be better once you give me something for this cold," she smiled at her.

She sat down. "Did you bring anyone with you?" she asked her.

"No, should I have?" she really became alarmed.

"Well, I think so. Is there someone you can call?" she asked Keysha.

She put her hands over her chest. Keysha started to feel sick to her stomach.

"Wait a minute, Doc. What is wrong with me?" she asked her quickly.

"Keysha, you know I've always been straight with you," she said.

"I know this. What is wrong with me? Am I going to die?" she demanded.

"Well, Keysha, we're all going to die at some point. But yes you do have a disease that has no cure at this time," she informed her.

"Oh my Lord, I have cancer," she fell to the floor.

"No, Keysha, you don't have cancer."

"Thank God for that. Then what else is there?" she asked the doctor.

"Keysha," she puts her hands on her shoulder, "You have AIDS."

The room went silent and Keysha was just frozen in time.

"I have AIDS? This can't be true! I always use protection and I don't do drugs. You

have to run the test again!" she yelled.

"Keysha, I ran the test several times. I wanted to be sure that it wasn't a false positive. Listen, Keysha, there are a couple of things we have to do. I'll start you on some medication and I need all the names of the people you have had sex with. Past and present lovers," she explained to her

"I never slept with anyone unprotected," she told her.

"What about oral sex? Have you gotten drunk lately and just don't remember?" she asked her.

"I don't give oral doc. I receive it. I never give," she said. Then she paused and had a flash back about the night of Monique's birthday party six or so months ago; the guy she woke up in bed with.

"Several months ago I got drunk and woke up in bed with someone. He is the only one," she told her.

"Well, you need to contact him and make him aware of what's going on. Tell him to get tested," she demanded. "Keysha, people live

perfectly normal lives with HIV."

"No disrespect, Dr. D, but my life has been anything but normal," she told her.

Keysha walked out of the office and on to the street in total disbelief. She quickly picked up the phone to call her cousin.

"Monique Williams speaking, how may I help you?" she answered.

"Monique, I need to see you right now," Keysha was crying hysterically.

"What's the matter, Keysha? Something happen at the doctors?" she asked her.

"Yes, yes, please, come get me from downtown!" she told her.

"I can't get off. I just got here," she told her.

"Monique, it's an emergency. I need to talk to you," she said crying, wiping her nose.

"Well, let's talk right now on the phone," she suggested.

"No, Monique, I can't."

"Okay. Okay. I can leave in a couple of hours. Catch the bus to my house and use the keys I gave you. Wait for me there," she said.

"Thank you. I love you."

Keysha saw the bus coming and she ran over to catch it. She was sitting on the bus crying and shaking. Everyone was looking at her like she was a nut. The bus finally pulled up to her stop and she got off. Keysha walked over to Monique's apartment, took out the keys and let herself in. Once in the apartment she sat on the sofa and started crying again.

"What's wrong with you? One of your men dump your ass?" Davon asked her.

"Davon, don't start with me today."

"As a matter of fact, how the hell did you get in here?"

"Monique gave me a key."

"What!"

"Davon, shut the fuck up. Don't nobody want to hear you're bitching and whining."

"Man, get the fuck out of my house," he told her.

"I'm not going anywhere. By the way the way, where is your cousin, Malcolm, from the party, what is his phone number?" she asked.

"What party?" Davon played dumb.

"Davon, the party where I whipped your ass," she reminded him.

"Oh, yeah. Why?" he smiled.

"Well, I need his phone number."

"For what? You didn't get enough in your mouth that night?" he said

"You are a true bastard," she yelled at him.

"Why? Are you feeling sick?"

Keysha turned around and looked at him. What the fuck was he talking about?

"What did you say?" she asked him

"Are you feeling sick? You have a cold, achy and purple spots everywhere?" He started laughing.

"You set him up to infect me!"

"You're fucking right. I knew that you would fuck him, considering you're a project whore. I asked him to help me get rid of you. He gladly helped."

"What kind of person are you?" she asked him.

They started arguing and cussing each other out and Monique walked in the door.

"Stop. Stop. What is going on? I could hear the both of you all the way downstairs," she asked them.

"Nothing, baby. Your cousin is tripping again," he quickly answered.

"Oh, I'm not tripping Monique. Let me tell you what Davon has done," she tried to tell her.

"Shut the fuck up. I outta punch you in your face. But I might get sick," he said to her.

"Wait. Stop this shit now. Keysha what's going on?" Monique asked her.

"The nasty bitch has AIDS," Davon blurted out.

Monique just stood there in shock. "Keysha, what is he talking about?" She asked.

"He is telling the truth. That's why I've been sick lately. And Dr. D told me today. Davon was in on it the whole time," I said.

"Keysha, I swear if you try to break up my family, I will kill you before the AIDS will." Davon looked at her.

"Davon, shut up," Monique said. "What does he have to do with it?"

"You remember the night of the party when me and Davon got into it?" she asked.

"Yeah, I remember," she said.

"Well, Davon's cousin took me home and I was drunk. He had sex with me, unprotected, and he was the one who infected me with AIDS," she told her.

"But what does that have to with Davon? It's not like he knew. Did you Davon?" she asked. But he didn't answer her.

"Not only did he know, he asked his cousin to infect me so that I would be out of your life," she told her.

She walked over to Davon and punched him in the face. He tried to hold her, but she just went berserk on him.

"You want to take the only person in this world, besides my mother and daughter, I love, away from me?" she said.

"Monique, baby, let's talk about it. We can work past this," he begged.

"No, we can't. The wedding's off. I want

you out of here," she said

"The wedding's Saturday, Monique. Fuck that whore," he said

"Davon, get out of here," she said. Then she walked over to the sofa and was just holding her.

"Let me tell you about your wonderful cousin," he said. "I also fucked your cousin." Monique looked at me to see if I was going to deny it.

"You're always saying that Harmony and Treasure look so much alike. They should, since they're half-sisters. Now ask your cousin why she didn't tell you that," he said to Monique.

"Keysha, please tell me he is lying," Monique begged.

"He's not, Monique. Let me explain," Keysha said. She jumped up and looked at her like she was dirt.

"Damn, Keysha all those years I defended you. It was all true. You would fuck anybody with a dick. And now you got caught

in your own web and have to pay the ultimate price. Your life. I guess it's true what they say. Like mother, like daughter. "Monique said to her. That cut her like a knife. Keysha wanted to be nothing like her mother.

"Yeah, you nasty bitch," Davon said to her

"Nasty? You're just as nasty as she is. Take me to court, because your daughter won't see you anytime soon." Monique stated. "Now both of you get the fuck out of my house and my life."

As the door slammed behind Keysha she could here Monique crying. Davon didn't leave when she did. She could hear him begging her not to leave him and Monique was screaming. This has had to be the worst day of her life.

CHAPTER 14

This had been the month from hell. Monique found out Keysha slept with Davon. She got fired and never started college. Oh, yeah, the biggest of all, Keysha was dying from AIDS.

Keysha was lying in bed and Treasure's knocked at the door, crying. She didn't feel like being bothered. She was depressed and wished she could wake from this nightmare. Keysha had tried to call Monique all month long but she wouldn't return her calls. She really fucked up.

"Mommy, can I come in?" Treasure cried out.

"Yes, Boo-Boo," she said. She opened the door and picked her up.

Keysha walked to the kitchen and got some eggs and bacon to cook Treasure some breakfast. She sat Treasure in her booster seat. She reached in the cabinet to get the grits. Keysha sat the breakfast on the table so her daughter could eat. Keysha sat on the sofa. She began to cry again.

Knowing that she would not see her daughter grow up was killing her. She didn't even have anyone to leave her to. Keysha reached for the remote and turned the TV on. Maury Povich was on and the topic was about attempted murder with your body. This was ironic, because the lady on the show got AIDS from her boyfriend. She took him to court. He was convicted of attempted murder and was serving a life sentence. His brother was also in jail on conspiracy charges. He knew his brother had AIDS, but never said anything.

"Black and Davon. I got your asses," she said out loud.

Keysha got up, grabbed Treasure out of the high chair and got dressed to take her to her aunt's for the day. Monique had not told her what was going on yet.

Keysha came back to the apartment. She took the phone book and looked for any attorney. She found one and called.

"Hello. Jamison and Jamison. Tinea Wilson. How may I help you?" the secretary asked.

"Yes. I would like to set up a consultation meeting with one of your lawyers," Keysha told her.

"May I ask what it pertains to?" she asked.

"I'd rather say at the consultation, if that's okay."

"No problem. I have an opening today at three. Is that too soon?" she asked.

"No, not at all," Keysha said.

"Good. Your appointment is with Michael Taylor," the secretary said.

"I'll be there," she said.

"Okay, let me get your name," she asked her.

"Keysha Williams."

"Ms. Williams, we will see you at three," she said.

Great. She would definitely have the last word on this matter. Now she had to go to the closet to get out her professional clothes. When this lawyer saw her, Keysha wanted him to know she meant business.

She grabbed her purse and headed

downtown. While in the car she started to wonder. Will this be in the news? She hoped not and wait until her mother found out. Traffic was horrible but she finally reached the building. The building was beautiful and very tall. She went in. The office was on the fifth floor. Keysha ran for the elevator and a whole bunch of stiff shirts were in there. She got off and walk towards the office.

"Hello. I have a three o'clock appointment with Mr. Taylor," she said

"Oh, yes, Ms. Williams. Have a seat and I'll let him know you're here," she said.

A gorgeous, tall black man came out of the office. He had a cream white suit on that was tailored to perfection.

"Keysha. Keysha Williams," he said.

"Yes, Mr. Taylor. I'm Mrs. Williams," she said.

"It's me, Keysha. Mike," he said.

"Mike," I said. She really didn't remember him. Oh, God, she hoped this wasn't someone she had fucked before.

"Kingdom Cum," he whispered in her

ear.

"Oh, Mike. How are you?" she said to him. Damn who would have ever thought that he was a high powered attorney? Freaks come in every form.

"Well, come on into my office," he motioned to her.

"Thanks," she said

His office was bananas. It had huge windows, leather sofas, and a huge flat- screen TV. This man was living the life. Keysha wished she had done things differently.

"So, what brings you in today?" he asked her.

"Well a friend of mine is having a problem with a guy," she said to him. Keysha really didn't know how to tell this story.

"Just tell me exactly what is going on. Nothing shocks me," he said

"Well, my friend was infected by a man with AIDS. The man knew that he had it and intentionally gave it to her. Also, the man's cousin set the whole thing up," she told him.

"Damn. I am shocked," he said.

"I thought nothing shocked you?" Keysha said.

"Well, there is always a first. Okay, your friend needs a criminal lawyer for that shit," he said.

"Well, can you help her?" she asked

"Yeah, but she will have to come in herself," he said.

"I'll try and convince her," she said

"It's not Monique, is it?" he asked, looking scared.

"No, it's not her," she laughed.

"Okay. I have a friend who can get everything started. But first you will have to go on a dinner date with me," he said.

"I don't think so," she said.

"Why? Because I slept with Monique?" he asked.

"Partly," she said

Before he could say anything one of his partners walked in.

"Hey, Mike." He stopped and looked at her. "I didn't know you were with a client."

"I was about to call you," he said

"Keysha Williams. This is the attorney I was referring to. This is Joshua Daniels, my partner," Mike said.

"Hi, Joshua. It's nice to meet you," she said

Joshua was your typical white boy. So Keysha thought until she overheard Mike and his conversation.

"Bye, Ms. Williams, it was nice to have met you." He smiled.

"Mike, can I talk to you in the hallway?" he asked him.

"Yeah," Mike said

"Excuse us," Joshua said to her. When they got up to talk, Keysha tip-toed to the door to listen to their conversation.

"Yo. She is fine as shit," Joshua said. "Does she get down with white boys?"

"I don't know. But what I do know is that she is a nasty freak," Mike said to him.

"How do you know?" he asked

"Remember that party I did? It was her cousin's bachelorette party," he said

"The one where you fucked the shit out

of? The bride to be?" he asked

"The very one," Mike smiled.

"So what does she want, or do I even have to ask?" Joshua nudged him.

"She wants me to work on a case for her, but it doesn't matter. I'm not really going to help her. She can't afford our services, but I want to fuck her.

"So let's pretend and see if we can both get those panties." Mike gave Joshua dap.

Keysha rushed back to her seat. She was so pissed off.

Keysha could not believe how they were talking about her. But she had something for their asses.

"Sorry we took so long. Going over another case. You know the privacy act." He smiled at her.

"Of course I do," she said

"Well, Joshua said he would take your case," Mike said to her.

"Really? Thank you." Keysha faked a smile. "I can't wait to tell my girlfriend. She will be relieved."

"No problem, Keysha." Joshua said.

"Hey, Keysha, you think you could meet Joshua and me at my house? Go over the strategy for your friend's problem?" He looked at her.

"At your house? What's up with that?" she asked him. It's not like she didn't already know.

"It's not like that. We just want to be in a comfortable environment," Joshua said.

"I guess that would be okay," she said to the both of them.

"Well, let me give you my address. Can you come around seven?" Mike asked her.

"I sure can. I'll see you boys then." She took the piece of paper and walked out.

Keysha got in her car and thought to herself. Men are shit. Always thinking with their dicks. Since Mike and Joshua wanted to treat her like a whore, a whore is what they would get.

But, boy, in the long run, wouldn't they be sorry. She reached in her purse and grabbed the cell phone. Keysha called her aunt to see if

Treasure could stay the night and she said yes.

Once Keysha got home. She stood in her living room, realizing she had nothing to offer the world she lived in. She stood there. Keysha debated killing herself. She thought of her daughter. She decided against that idea. She knew what she had to do and tonight Mike and Joshua will be the first to taste the wrath of Keysha.

She pulled up to the address that Mike had given her. The neighborhood was a gated community. She had to get buzzed in just to enter. Keysha had to admit Mike was living large. She walked up to the condo doors.

"Damn, another button."

"Hello?" Mike answered.

"Hey, Mike, it's Keysha."

"Come on up. It's the door on the second floor, letter C," he said.

Keysha walked in and there was an elevator to the second floor. This nigga was livin large. She hated him. Keysha got off the elevator and Mike was already standing in the hallway. He was nothing but a horny little

bastard.

"Hey," she said and gave him a hug.

"Come on in," he said to her.

"Hi, Keysha." Joshua said.

"Hi, Joshua."

The house was right out of a magazine. He had a marble fireplace, high cathedral ceilings and Italian leather sofas. Keysha was in amazement at how well he kept up the place.

"Let me take your coat," Joshua said to her.

"Thank you."

"Would you like a drink?" Mike asked her.

"Sure, why not?" she said.

"Well, let's get down to your case. Mike has told me everything about your friend. I need to let you know right up front it is going to be very expensive," Joshua said.

"Well, she doesn't have a lot of money. I don't know how she is going to pay for it. Can't you do it pro bono?" she asked

"We are only allowed one of those a year. And we have already done that," Mike

said to her.

Keysha took a sip of her wine. She walked over to the fireplace and looked at the fire.

"Maybe she could make some kind of payments."

"No, that won't work. You're going to have to put down ten percent. That will be about twenty five G's," Joshua said.

"So, what can I do to insure she gets the help she needs?" she asked.

Mike looked at Joshua. Then they both looked at Keysha, and she knew the proposition was coming.

"Well if you allow Joshua and me to have sex with you, we will figure out a way to take your case for free," Mike said.

"But I thought you said you couldn't do it for free," she said.

"Well, if you work with us, we'll work with you," Joshua's pasty white ass said.

"I guess I don't have a choice," she said to them.

"Well, should we get started?" Mike

asked her.

Joshua started taking off his clothes. She walked over to him and started kissing him. Keysha bent down.

She grabbed his dick, and believe it or not, he had a nice size dick. He was moaning and pulling her head back and forth. Mike came over and stood her up. He was already naked. He undressed her. Mike pushed her on the sofa. He then opened her legs and started licking her pussy. Joshua stood over top of her and put his dick in Keysha's mouth.

"It's my time to get some of that black pussy," Joshua said to Mike.

"Handle your business," Mike told him.

Mike got up and sat on the opposite sofa. Joshua grabbed her hand. He took Keysha over by the fireplace and laid her on the rug. He put her legs over her head and started to fuck her. She couldn't let this white bitch think he was killing this pussy. She turned him over and rode the shit out of him.

"You like black pussy, do you?" she said to him while tearing his dick up.

"Oh, yeah, Keysha. I love black pussy," he said.

Keysha had that bitch telling her he loved her. He finally came. Mike walked over to Keysha.

"My turn, brother," he said to Joshua.

He took her hand and they went in his room. Now remember, this nigga had a ten-inch dick.

"Get up on the bed and let me wet my dick," he told her.

She climbed up on his huge four-post bed. There were candles everywhere. He pulled her closer to the end of the bed.

He put his big dick in Keysha. He pulled his penis back and forth, slowly.

"Oh, yeah, this shit feels good. I knew you were the one. I wanted to fuck you at that party, but you didn't give me the time of day. Well, I'm in this pussy now," he said while moaning.

Mike was a freak. He took hot wax and poured it on her. He spit in Keysha's pussy, then licked it. She almost got sick. Joshua's

sperm was still in her. Mike didn't care; he just wanted to treat her like a whore. He told Keysha to relax while he stuck his 10-inch dick in her ass. Keysha screamed, and he put a pillow over her face. He went deep and hard. When he was finished she was bleeding.

"Don't worry about the blood, Keysha. It's because I have a big dick. You're not the first one to bleed from this dick." He said it like he was the shit.

Keysha got up. She was in so much pain, she could barely walk.
"Can I take a shower, Mike?" she asked him.

"No, I don't think so. I don't need a bitch smell in my house. I don't want my girlfriend to kill me," he said and then walked in the bathroom and shut the door.

She heard the shower running. So she limped to the living room and put her clothes on. Joshua was passed out on the floor where she left him. Keysha pushed the down button on the elevator. She walked out to her car and eased her ass onto the seat. She would have to go home and soak in some Epsom salt. It was

agony the whole ride home, but she finally reached the house.

Keysha ran a hot bubble bath. She sat down in the tub. Keysha cried because she was in so much pain. After sitting in the tub for an hour she finally got out. She went to the kitchen and put some ice in a bag. Keysha crawled in the bed and put the bag between her legs. She popped three Tylenol PM and finally went to sleep.

Keysha's alarm clock went off and she got out of bed. Her ass was still very sore. She got dressed and headed out to get her daughter.

On the way out she stopped by the flower shop. She pulled up to her Aunt's house and parked right beside Monique's car. Keysha was hoping that Monique would talk to her.

"Hi, Aunt Jackie. Thanks for keeping Treasure last night," Keysha said

"You know I love having her over here," she said.

Monique came down the steps. She stopped and looked at Keysha.

"Mom, I get off work today at four o'clock," Monique said.

"Hi, Monique." Keysha said.

"I know you're not talking to me," Monique said.

"What is going on between the two of you?" her aunt asked.

"Nothing. Except Keysha slept with Davon," Monique told her mother.

"Keysha did what? Did some of those jealous hoochies tell you that? Those two can't even stand each other!" her aunt said.

"Tell her, Keysha, or do you want me to?" Monique said.

"Auntie, it's true," she said in a pathetic voice.

"Why, Keysha? Why ruin the relationship you have with your cousin?" she asked her.

"Oh, yeah, that shit is definitely ruined," Monique said.

"Moe, it doesn't have to be this way!" Keysha begged her.

"You should have thought about it

before you fucked my man. And then you had the nerve to go and have a baby with him," She said.

"Keysha? Treasure is Davon's child?" her aunt asked her.

"Yes, Mom. Harmony and Treasure are sisters." Monique said

Her Aunt just looked at her. She was so disappointed in Keysha.

"I'll get Treasure and leave." She said.

"She's upstairs playing with her sister," Monique said, before walking out the door.

Keysha got back to her house. Treasure fell asleep on the way home and she put her in the bed. Keysha got in her bed and fell asleep.

Across town, Mike and Joshua were in the office bragging on the night they had together.

"Man, I tore that pussy up last night," Joshua said.

"You might have tore the pussy up, but I tore that asshole to pieces," Mike said.

"And she really thought we were going to help a whore like that," Joshua said.

"Hey, my girlfriend is leaving for the weekend again. Let's have another session with Keysha," Mike suggested.

"Yeah, her dumb ass will do it. You know, to help her friend." They laughed

There was a knock at the door. The secretary came in with a bouquet of flowers.

"These came for the both of you," she said.

"For both of us?" Mike questioned.

"Yes. The two of you must be special," she said

"Thank you, Mrs. Wilson," Mike said

"Maybe we should tag team Mrs. Wilson next," Joshua said.

"We don't mess around in the work place," Mike said

Mike and Joshua looked at the beautiful flowers.   They noticed the note attached to them.

"Hey, there is a note," Mike said.

"Read it," Joshua said.

"I just wanted to thank you guys for last night," Mike said.

"I guess we made a lasting impression last night. What else does it say?" Joshua asked.

"I knew from the beginning that you were not going to help me. But I wanted to teach the two of you a lesson. I just wanted to welcome you, Michael Taylor, and you, Joshua Daniels, to the wonderful world of AIDS," he said with his mouth open.

"AIDS? Are you serious? I thought she said her friend had it," Joshua said.

"I can't believe it. She has to be lying," Mike said

"I can't have it. I have a wife at home and three children," Joshua said.

"I'm calling the police," Mike said.

* * * * *

Keysha was lying in bed when she heard sirens outside. She started to wonder who the hell they were the coming for. It sounded like ten of them. What the hell is that? There was a loud bang on the door.

"Who is it?" she asked.

"It's the police," the officer said.

She opened the door. There were five police officers at her door. Her daughter ran up and hugged her leg.

"Ms. Williams?" he asked.

"Yes," she answered him.

"You're under arrest for the attempted murder of Michael Taylor and Joshua Daniels," he said to her.

The officer read Keysha her rights. He placed handcuffs on her. They didn't even let her put on shoes. A female officer was there, too, and she took Keysha's daughter to the back of the house.

"What will happen to my daughter?" she asked him.

"She will go into foster care, unless a family member comes forward to take her," he told Keysha. She came out of her apartment. There were cameras and people everywhere. The officer walked her to the car and slammed the door.

CHAPTER 15

Well Keysha couldn't have fucked her life up any more than this. She has been in jail for nine months now. Her trial was last week and today is her sentencing. Keysha had no one in her corner. Monique would not speak to her. Keysha called her mother to see if she could get Treasure out of foster care. Pamela immediately told Keysha that she had no daughter, therefore, she had no granddaughter.

"Ms. Williams, the judge is ready for you," the officer said.

Keysha stood up and stumbled. She forgot she had shackles on her feet. Keysha entered the courtroom. Sitting behind the prosecuting attorney were Michael and Joshua. There was also Nathan, her old boss, and Travis, the rental manager. They had all testified against her.

"Ms. Williams, please stand," the judge said. "You have been found guilty of attempted murder of the four gentlemen sitting to the

right of you. The jury has agreed on a sentence. Keysha Williams, you are sentenced to twenty-five years to life without the possibility of parole."

She couldn't believe it. Keysha couldn't hear anything. Travis was hugging his mother. Nathan took off towards Keysha, but the officer stopped him in time.

"Ms. Williams I know you were wronged. That is no reason to take the life of other's," the judge said.

The officer came and handcuffed her. He started to walk Keysha out the side door. She looked up. In the back of the courtroom was Monique. She had shades on. She took them off and she was crying. She did still care about her.

* * * * *

It had been a year and a half. Keysha wondered every day, if she would have done things differently, how her life would be. She would have her daughter, her cousin and she would be a college graduate by now.

"Hey, bitch," the other inmate said.

"What? Who the fuck are you talking to?" Keysha asked.

In Keysha's cell there were five big bitches standing, blocking her way. She had already fought numerous times in here. Her cellmate was at a parole hearing. She guessed she would have to handle this shit herself.

"I'm talking to you, bitch," the husky one said.

"Looks like she wants some," the black crispy one said.

"Looking for what?" she asked.

"Looking to get your ass whipped." She stepped closer to her. Keysha reached under her pillow and grabbed a shank she made. She jumped down off the top bunk.

"Bitch, I'll cut you right where you stand," she yelled out.

"What? Now you're going cut me, cunt?"

"Hurry up, Brass. Here comes her buddy," the look-out said

"I got your ass later, bitch," Brass said.

A breath of momentary relief. Charlotte backed in and the correctional officer took the cuffs off her. She climbed in her bunk.

"How did it go?" Keysha asked.

"How the fuck you think it went?" She snapped at her.

"Damn, bite a bitch's head off," Keysha said.

"What the fuck you say?" she sat up.

Keysha knew right then to shut up. Charlotte was built just like a man. She acted like one, too. Keysha learned that the first night in there, when she tried to pop off at the mouth with her. She broke her ribs, and Keysha was in the infirmary for two weeks.

"Nothing, Charlotte," Keysha lowered her voice.

"I came in just in time," she said.

"Why you say that?"

"Brass was about to take that pussy," she laughed

"She wasn't about to take shit," Keysha said.

"She wants you bad. I could help you,

but I don't feel like it," she said to her.

Just then four correctional officers came up. It was going to be a shake down. Brass had snitched Keysha out.

"Get your asses up against the wall," he said

"For fucking what now?" Charlotte asked.

"This really doesn't concern you, Charlotte." He said

Charlotte had a lot of connections in there. She pimped other inmates to the correctional officers. They have been trying to get Keysha for months now. She didn't know how much longer she could hold out. Charlotte looked at Keysha and smiled.

"Inmate Williams, get up against the wall and turn around," he said.

The other officers came in and searched her bunk. One searched Keysha and was just feeling her up. Then they found the shank.

"Well, who does this belong to?" the officer asked her.

"The shit ain't mines," Charlotte said.

"It's not mine, either," Keysha said.

"Oh, it's not?" Charlotte looked at her.

"I don't know how it got here," Keysha lied.

"Somebody's going to pay for this," he said. "Okay, guys. You can leave. We have everything we need. Looks like Brass is going to have a new roommate." He smiled at her.

Keysha did not want to be transferred to Brass's area. She climbed on the bunk and wondered how she would get out of this shit. Keysha looked up. Charlotte and the officer were talking and laughing like they were old buddies. Then she came over.

"Do you want me to help you?" she asked.

"What do I have to do?" Keysha asked her.

"Well, Jenkins wants to fuck you," she said.

"I can do that," she told her.

"Oh, that's just the beginning." She looked at Keysha.

"What else?"

"You are now to be my house bitch. This means you do what I say. If I say eat my pussy, you better jump up and do it. You also will clean our house and wash our clothes. Also, whenever Jenkins wants you, he can have you. Like right now," she told her.

"Alright," Keysha said. She had hit rock bottom.

"Come with me, Williams," the officer said.

He handcuffed her and walked her down to the showers.

"Get on your knees," he ordered her.

"Are you going to take the handcuffs off me?"

"For what? You're only going to use your mouth," he said.

Keysha got on her knees and began sucking his dick until he came in her mouth. He didn't even let Keysha clean up. He took his dick and wiped it on her jumpsuit.
She got up and he walked her back to the cell were Charlotte was waiting for her.

"Charlotte, next Friday. I'll come back to

get her," he said. Then he walked over to her. He handed her a pack of cigarettes.

"No problem. She'll be ready," she said.

She took her cigarettes and put them up. Keysha climbed up in her bunk.

"Get your ass down and brush your teeth. I don't like my bitches dirty."

Keysha got down. Brushed her teeth and cleaned herself up. She turned around and Charlotte was lying there naked. She had her legs spread eagle.

"My pussy is throbbing. Take care of that," she commanded.

She didn't want to, but she belonged to her now. Keysha bent down and started licking. She thought if she did a bad job, she would leave her alone.

"Bitch, don't make me fuck you up. You better eat my pussy like your life depended on it," she told her

Keysha ate the hell out of her pussy. She had her moaning and climbing the walls. Keysha was so scared she would beat her.

Afterwards Keysha got cleaned up again. She climbed in her bunk and cried until she fell asleep.

"Hey, Williams, you have mail," the correctional officer yelled.

Mail? Keysha never got mail. She wondered who it was from. She was just happy to have some contact with the outside world. She walked over to the bars. The officer handed her the opened letter.

"Damn, I can't open my own shit?" she said.

"You know the rules." He said.

She looked down at the envelope. It was from Monique. She started to shake. Keysha opened the letter.

Dear Keysha:

It has been over two years and I feel I could talk to you now. I wish every day that things could be different. Regardless of what you did to me, I still love you. I had to think about what you went through as a child. And what you're going through now. After you got sentenced. I had a hard time coping with that. I want you to know. I was at all of your hearings. I went to a lawyer

and told him what happened with Black and Davon. Payback's a bitch because both will be tried for what they did to you. So expect a call from an attorney. I know it's nothing compared to your sentence. Also I have bad news. Aunt Pam and Colin were killed by Colin's wife a couple of weeks ago. She caught them in bed at one of their summer homes, but in the mix of all the tragedies to our family, something good came out of it. The day they took Treasure to a foster home two years ago, I went that same day and got her out of there. She's been with my mom and me ever since. I just want you to know I adopted her. I plan on raising her and Harmony together as sisters. Well, I have to go. I just wanted you to know your daughter is fine. I'll write soon.

I love you always, Monique

P.S. I hope you like the picture Treasure drew you.

She couldn't believe it. She had Treasure. Treasure drew a picture of them holding hands and walking into the sunset.

"Who is that from?" Charlotte asked.

"My family," she told her.

"Oh really? I'm your family now," she reminded Keysha.

The bells went off in the facility. It was time for roll call.

"Roll call, everybody," the CO said.

"Inmate number 22569874"

"Here," she answered.

Keysha had been in here going on eight years and had been passed around like a roll of toilet tissue. Every week she was fucking someone or washing someone's nasty ass drawers. Keysha still belonged to Charlotte and now she wanted to marry her off to Brass. She had managed to stay clear of her all these years. Keysha didn't want to think about that right now. Her daughter was coming to see her today, and Monique, too. The visits are all that kept her from going crazy in here, but Treasure is eleven years old and doesn't want to have anything to do with her. Keysha wanted to make things right with her. She tried to make herself look presentable for her daughter's visit. She tried to hides the bald spots she had gotten from being in continuous fights. Keysha began to cry and wondered why she was going through this.

"What the fuck is your problem?"

"Charlotte, I don't feel like it today."

"That's cool. Brass will be waiting on you

276

after your visit."

Keysha walked out of the cell. As she walked down the narrow cold hall she began to feel even more depressed. What could she do to avoid becoming Brass's lover? It would have to wait. Her baby was waiting on her. Her heart began to pound as if it were the first time she had ever seen her child. She wished things could be different, but the reality is, they were not. She reached the glass window where she could see the families. Keysha sees Monique but not Treasure. She began to panic.

"Where is my daughter?"

"She did not want to come."

"Why not?"

"Keysha, I really don't want to go into that."

"Look, I don't want to argue with you, but that is my child and I deserve to know why she doesn't want to see me."

"She has been going to a therapist."

"For what?"

"Do you really have to ask why?"

"No, I don't."

"She is really going through it. The nightmares, the depression, the constant teasing at school."

Keysha began to cry. She did not want this for her child. Those same feelings she was having about her life began to flood back again.

"You know what? Fuck it."

"Why are you acting like that?"

"I don't need any of your shit. I will be here for the rest of my motherfucking life. Like I said fuck y'all."

She got up and headed for the door. Monique was stunned by it all. She couldn't understand why she was acting like that. The reason her daughter was stressed is because of all the shit she had done.

"Keysha, stop!"

Keysha walked straight through the doors and never looked back. When she passed the last set of steel doors it was decided she was to become a new bitch. No more following no one's rules! Fuck being a house bitch and start beating bitches asses.

She walks into her cell and hops up on her

bunk.

"So, Bitch, how was your visit."

"Charlotte, if I was you, I would shut the fuck up."

"Bitch, don't let your little visit get you beat the fuck down."

"Oh, really?"

Keysha jumped off the bunk and punch Charlotte in the throat. When Charlotte went to grab her throat. Keysha began to kick her and stomp her face. She then snatched her calendar off the wall. Behind this was a little hold where she kept a little shank. Keysha began to jab her in the back continuously.

"Bitch, I run the show now, and you will be eating my pussy."

"Fuck you."

"Oh? Fuck me? No, Bitch. Fuck you."

The guards ran in and pulled Keysha off Charlotte. There was blood everywhere and the guards are very thrown by it all. She never showed any signs of this. Keysha continued to act crazy because she knew once she saw the psychiatric counselor they would go easier on

her. She kept kicking and screaming.

"I'm tired of having to fuck everyone in here. Charlotte, the guards and anyone who she sells me to."

One guard looked at her in amazement. He did not know that she was having sex with his partner. The partner knew if this got out that his life would be ruined. So he took Keysha to the side to talk to her.

"What do you want?"

"I want that bitch out of my fucking cell."

"Cool. I will make sure it is her who takes the blame for this."

"No more fucking you or anybody. I want you to get me some weed and I want you and your boys to beat and fuck the shit out of Brass."

"Beat her up but fuck her? Hell no."

"Why? You fuck me, and I have AIDS?"

"Well, so do I."

Keysha was silent. Why would a man go around and infect other people. Well that's

what happened to her. She thought to herself that she would get his ass to before it was all over.

"I don't really give a damn about you. Just do like I said."

He took Keysha back to her cell. The guard told his boy that everything was cool. Charlotte was gone when she got back. They started taking all her stuff out of the cell. She began to think this was the beginning of a lot of fun. The guard came towards her.

"She is gone and will be transferred elsewhere."

"Good."

"As far as Brass, that will be taken care of tonight."

The next morning at role call she saw Brass. She had a black eye, tape on her fingers, which looked broken and a profoundly limp. Keysha was extremely happy by it all. All of a sudden she had more friends than she could count, if that's what you want to call it. Now all of a sudden, bitches wanted to wash her drawers and be her main bitch. She wasn't a

lesbian but started to fall for temptation.

"Keysha, you have a new cell mate," the guard said

"Oh yeah. What up, Bitch?"

"What's poppin?"

"Your ass will be soon."

The girl just stood there looking very frighten. Keysha had definitely changed over the last eight years. She had no regard for life and will fuck you up at the drop of a dime. Keysha ran her block. She sold drugs, bitches and protection. She used to be at the bottom of the barrel, now she is at the top of the heap.

"What's your name, Bitch?"

"T."

"Your real name."

"Treasure."

Keysha just stared at her. She began to think of her own child who was eighteen now. She had not seen her since she was ten. Keysha had refused all contact with Monique and Treasure. Her heart was so hardened by being rejected by her daughter.

"Are you going to hurt me?"

"No, dumb ass."

Keysha decided right there to take this one under her wings. She thought that maybe this was a sign from God. Normally not very religious, at this moment she was. Keysha would show her the ropes of inmate life. She could tell that she was real green. This girl was real upscale. Manicured nails, shaped eyebrows and gorgeous hair. She obviously took great care of herself and when locked up, that is a target ready to be taken.

"What are you in for?"

"Holding weight for my man."

"Damn, you are stupid as you look."

"I loved him."

"And where is he at?"

"I said I loved him. Past tense!"

"That motherfucker is laid up in another bitch's ass."

The girl sat on the bottom bunk and began to cry. She really thought this fool truly loved her. Keysha put her arms on her shoulder to comfort her.

"I'm not no dike."

"Don't no body want your ass. Believe me, if I did, I would have your ass."

"I'm sorry. I'm not no hard type of bitch."

"Oh, you will be."

Keysha decided to take Treasure under her wing and teach her the ropes. First, she let her know that she ran shit in there. Keysha taught her how to fight, manipulate and sell drugs. Treasure soaked it all up and began to enjoy the power.

"Bitch, where is Keysha's money at?"

"I will get it to her soon," the scared inmate said.

"Oh, that will be too little too late."

With Keysha standing right there, Treasure began to whip her ass. Next Keysha's other flunkies jumped in. Keysha loved the loyalty she got from her.

There was something about her; she felt like her mother and was trying to fill the void of missing her daughter. She figured it was a sign from God, them having the same name. After the fight, Keysha and Treasure went back to the

cell.

"Damn! I fucked that bitch up."

"Yes, you did."

"You taught me well, and I love you for that."

"What is a mother for?"

"You are so right."

"Hey, later on, do you want to go to the library?"

"For what?"

"To escape all the drama for a while."

"Yeah, why not?"

Treasure left to have her weekly visit and Keysha took a nap. While sleeping, Keysha had a dream that she was playing in a field of roses with her daughter. In the dream she noticed a flower rising up out of the ground and told her daughter to smell it. The flower opened and then suddenly closed and went back into the ground. She started awake in a cold sweat. Treasure walked in at that moment.

"You okay?"

"Yeah, I just had a dream about a rose opening and closing."

"Okay, why would that wake you up in a cold sweat like that?"

"Because that symbolizes the beginning and end of life."

"Okay, you are crazy. Are you ready to go to the library?"

"I don't know. I just have a bad feeling today. Maybe we should just stay in the cell today."

"Girl, come on."

"Okay."

She was very reluctant about going, but against her better judgment she went. Once in the library she got a chill down her back. Treasure took her to the back of the library and sat down at a table.

"Why are we all the way back here?"

"I don't know. This is where I sit when I come every day."

"Well, what do you want to read?"

"Sit and relax I will go get the books."

While sitting there Keysha's thoughts were on the dream she just had. She was wondering if her daughter was in trouble. She

promised herself that she would call her after she finished reading.

"Hey, Bitch!"

Keysha looked up.   It was the girl who just got beat up, Brass and the correctional officer. She knew she was in real trouble but Treasure and her could take them or at least survive the beating that was sure to come.

"What the fuck ya'll want?"

"That motherfucking ass."

Brass leapt onto Keysha and they began to fight. Next the girl who had just gotten beaten up earlier jumped in, but Keysha was still hanging in there. The CO did nothing.   He just stood there with a smile on his face. She looked past him and saw Treasure approaching the fight. She knew she was finally going to get some help.

"Get the fuck off her!"

Everyone jumped back and stopped beating on her. She was bloody from top to bottom but still ready to get up with her sidekick. Treasure walked toward Keysha, looking full of concern.

"I'm glad you got my back. These bitches are trying to kill me!"

"Yeah, I see."

"You ready to squad up?"

"And you know it."

Keysha stood up to finish the fight. Treasure turned and stabbed Keysha in the heart. Keysha was shocked.   She could not believe her daughter had stabbed her. She felt her life slipping away.

"Why? You are like my daughter!"

"I'm not your fucking daughter and by killing you the CO gets me out next week!"

"So you kill me to get your freedom."

"Your damn right.   I don't belong here."

Treasure looked at her and realized she has done the wrong thing. She only had three months left, which was tagged on because of all the fights Keysha kept her in. She looked at her lying in a pool of blood. Keysha motioned for her to come closer to her. By this time the library was empty. Brass, the CO and the beaten girl were gone. Treasure knelt down and put her head in her lap.

"I'm sorry Keysha."

"I don't blame you.   This place will change you."

Treasure began to cry and sob. The alarms rang and the guards rushed in. They began to question what happened. Treasure thought briefly about confessing the truth.

"What happened inmate?"

"It was...It was...." Treasure said.   "I don't know who did it."

They put Keysha on the stretcher and started to wheel her out. She motioned for Treasure to come closer.

"Do me one favor when you get out?"

"Anything."

"Tell my real daughter and my cousin, Monique, I will always love them."

Authors Contact Page

For purchases please contact me at

ligesaddler@outlook.com

www.ingramcontent.com/pod-product-compliance
Lightning Source LLC
Chambersburg PA
CBHW071306170626
46809CB00001B/352